PURRFECT LIFE

THE MYSTERIES OF MAX 42

NIC SAINT

PURRFECT LIFE

The Mysteries of Max 42

Copyright © 2021 by Nic Saint

All rights reserved. No part of this book may be reproduced in any form by any electronic or mechanical means including photocopying, recording, or information storage and retrieval without permission in writing from the author.

This is a work of fiction. Names, characters, places, brands, media, and incidents are either the product of the author's imagination or are used fictitiously. The author acknowledges the trademarked status and trademark owners of various products referenced in this work of fiction, which have been used without permission. The publication/use of these trademarks is not authorized, associated with, or sponsored by the trademark owners.

Edited by Chereese Graves

www.nicsaint.com

Give feedback on the book at: info@nicsaint.com

facebook.com/nicsaintauthor
@nicsaintauthor

First Edition

Printed in the U.S.A

PURRFECT LIFE

Baker Street Cats

My name is Dooley and I'm a ragamuffin. I'm also Max's best friend, and because he's my best friend, he asked me to write this introduction to our new mystery. I've never written an introduction before, so I hope you'll forgive me if it's not very good. Okay, let's begin. So first there was the woman who was murdered on the beach. Chase didn't know who killed her, and because he really wanted to find out, he went on television and asked people if they could help him.

Then there was the blackmail. A very nice woman named Rosa Bond was being blackmailed about a dark secret in her past, and so she asked Odelia to help her. And it worked. Well, more or less. The next day the blackmailer was found dead. The good news was that Rosa got her money back. The bad news was that he was murdered, which isn't very nice. Also, now we had to try and catch the killer, which is a lot of work. A lot of talking to a lot of people and asking them a lot of very personal questions. Good thing Chase is a cop. When people don't want to talk he can arrest them.

And then there was the boy who drowned in the pool.

And this is where I got confused. Was he murdered or not? Some people said he was, and others said that he wasn't. And for a while even Max didn't know, which is weird, since he's the smartest cat I know. Lucky for us (and for Rosa Bond) he finally figured it out. I just knew he would. Max is my hero. Even when things look pretty hopeless, and Chase has to go on television to ask people to help him, Max figures it out. I don't know how he does it. Brutus says it's because he has a big head. I don't know if that's true.

Well, I think that's it. I wanted to tell you who the murderer was but Max said I shouldn't. He says it would spoil the fun. I don't know what's so funny about murder, but then I guess Max knows best. Did I mention he's very clever? And now if you'll excuse me, I have some Discovery Channel to watch. There's a very interesting documentary on about tardigrades, also known as water bears or moss piglets. I think I'm going to enjoy that. Moss piglets. Is it a piece of moss that looks like a piglet or a piglet that likes to eat moss? I have absolutely no idea, but I'm going to find out!

CHAPTER 1

We were all gathered in the living room of the cozy little home we share with Odelia and her husband Chase, enjoying the evening watching television as we often do. Only this evening was special, since it was the first time Chase was to appear on TV.

For this auspicious occasion the whole clan had gathered: Odelia and Chase, of course, but also Odelia's mom and dad, and her grandmother. Even Uncle Alec was there, with his girlfriend Charlene, and Gran's friend Scarlett. In other words: we were entertaining a full house, and were lucky to have found ourselves a place right in front of the television, awaiting the big debut. With us I am of course referring to myself, but also to Dooley, my best friend and a Ragamuffin of the noblest kind, Harriet, a white Persian who belongs to Odelia's mom Marge, and Brutus, that black butch cat who belongs to Chase. Though let's not split hairs: in the Poole household, nobody actually belongs to anybody. In fact it wouldn't be unfair to say that we all belong to each other, since we all like to do what we can to further the investigations that have put Odelia on the crime-fighting map in

Hampton Cove, the small town on the East Coast we like to call home.

Another reason for the family to celebrate was that they'd finally managed to get rid of their house guest. Following one of my less inspired interventions, a man named Rudolph Vickery had been staying with us. He was Wilbur Vickery's brother, one of our local shopkeepers, and an aspiring musician, having chosen the heavy metal genre as a potential career path. Unfortunately he didn't possess a great deal of talent. Still, since he had now decided that to further his musical career he had to be in LA, we had wished him good luck—and in fact I think these good wishes came from the bottom of everyone's heart, since no one wanted to ever see the man's face again.

"Popcorn, anyone?" asked Uncle Alec, returning from the kitchen with two big bowls of steaming hot popcorn. "They're hot and fresh from the oven."

"You're making it sound as if we're going to watch an entire movie with Chase in the lead," Gran grumbled. "It's only a short interview, Alec. Blink and you'll miss it."

"It's Chase's big television premiere, Ma," said Uncle Alec as he let himself fall down onto the couch next to Charlene and handed her the second bowl.

"Did they make you wear makeup, honey?" asked Marge with a touch of concern in her voice. "I've heard that sometimes they put on so much makeup you end up looking completely different. It's to make sure you don't look shiny," she added as an explanation.

"No makeup," said Chase curtly as he dipped into the bowl of popcorn and sampled one or two kernels before settling back and fiddling with the remote.

"You see, when you're on TV, all your little skin blemishes are enhanced," Marge explained to the others, who weren't really listening. Charlene was checking her smartphone, no doubt making some last-minute important decisions, like whether to plant fuchsias or roses in the municipal flower beds—Charlene is the mayor of our town, you see, and always busy-busy-busy. And Scarlett, too, was smiling and tapping on her smartphone, presumably chatting with one of her many male admirers.

"Will you cut that out," Gran grumbled, taking her friend's phone away.

"Hey, I wasn't finished," Scarlett protested.

"You're finished now," said Gran. "It's Chase's big debut. And it doesn't happen every day that a member of this family is live on television."

"He won't be live, Ma," said Tex. He turned to his son-in-law. "When did you tape this, Chase?"

"This afternoon," said Chase. "Just after we found Josslyn Aldridge's body."

"So soon? But why?" asked Marge, who's always interested in the minutiae of Chase's police investigations. Being a librarian, she has an important role to play in the local community, providing fresh gossip to all who visit the library, which is a large contingent on normal days, and even more when a tragic event like a murder has taken place.

"It's probably a mugging gone wrong," said Uncle Alec. "And from experience we know that it's very difficult to solve cases like this, especially when there are no witnesses."

The woman Uncle Alec was referring to had been found on the beach by one of those people who like to go for a jog first thing in the morning. I'd never want to be seen dead going for a jog, especially that early, but then again I'm a cat. We don't go in for sports.

Josslyn Aldridge had been found next to a concrete staircase leading down from the boardwalk to the beach. The coroner ascertained that her head had been smashed against that concrete staircase. And since her purse was missing, and later found nearby, minus the woman's wallet, it stood to reason that the police was now looking for the mugger.

"Was she local?" asked Charlene, her business apparently concluded.

"A tourist," said Chase, who was heading up the investigation. "I talked to her friend, and they came down here for a one-week vacation, arriving in town two days ago."

"Oh, that's so sad," said Marge. "Where was she from?"

"Middletown, Ohio."

"And you have no idea who did this to her?" asked Tex with a frown. He seemed anxious to see his tax dollars not go to waste on fruitless police investigations.

"No, her friend told us that she happened to bump into an old work colleague that morning, and had arranged to have a drink, to talk about old times, but when she woke up this morning, and her friend's bed had not been slept in, she sounded the alarm."

"Do you think this colleague might have something to do with it?" asked Odelia.

"I doubt it," said Chase. "Like the Chief said, it's probably a mugging gone wrong. She must have met up with this colleague, then taken a stroll along the boardwalk when she ran afoul of a mugger who forced her down those steps where he proceeded to grab her purse. She must have put up a fight, and that's when he gave her a shove, her head hit the concrete steps, and when the mugger saw that she was dead, he panicked and ran off."

"Sad business," said Marge, shaking her head.

"And bad for tourism," Charlene added with a grim look on her face. "I hope you catch the bastard quickly, Alec."

"Oh, we will," Uncle Alec assured her.

"Ooh! It's about to start, you guys!" said Scarlett, pointing with one of her long-nailed fingers to the screen, where a picture of the unfortunate tourist had appeared, while the newscaster reiterated the events as Chase had already outlined them. Josslyn Aldridge was in her early sixties, with gray curly hair, and a sort of startled look on her face.

"Where did they get that horrible picture?" Marge muttered.

"We got it from her friend," said Chase. "It was the only one she could give us on such short notice."

And then the moment had come: Chase was on TV, being interviewed by a peppy young blonde, who seemed fresh out of school, holding a microphone under his nose.

"You were right, Chase, honey," said Marge. "They didn't use makeup."

"Look how shiny his face is," said Gran. "It looks like an ice skating rink."

"Gran is right, Max," said Dooley. "He does look very shiny."

"It was a warm day today, Dooley," I said. "And when humans sweat, they shine."

"I'm not sure makeup would have helped," said Scarlett. "It might have made things worse."

"Will you shut up," Uncle Alec growled. "You're missing Chase's big moment."

"So we'd like to ask that the colleague Josslyn had arranged to meet comes forward as soon as possible and gets in touch with us," Chase was saying on TV, looking straight into the camera now. "So we can reconstruct the last hours of her life, and hopefully catch the person responsible for this terrible crime."

"Don't you have a name for this colleague?" asked Marge.

Chase shook his head. "Josslyn never said, and Sadie didn't think it was important to ask."

"Sadie?"

"Josslyn's friend."

"Oh, right," said Marge.

"I think he looks good on screen," said Scarlett. "Don't you think he looks good on screen, Vesta?"

"His head looks big," said Gran.

"That's because he's on camera. They say the camera adds ten pounds."

"Well I think he looks great," said Odelia, patting her hubby on the arm. "In fact I think he looks amazing and he's doing a great job."

"Thanks, babe," Chase grunted.

"Why is he pulling at his nose, Max?" asked Dooley.

"Probably because he's nervous," said Brutus. "People who aren't used to being interviewed on camera always get nervous, and start doing stuff like pulling their noses or pulling their ears, or sweating and looking shiny."

We watched as Chase first pulled his nose, then pulled his ear, then pulled his nose again. All while looking very shiny indeed.

"He looks very shifty," said Harriet. "If I didn't know any better I would have thought he was the mugger."

"Yeah, well, the man is a cop, smoochie poo," said Brutus. "Not a professional actor."

"That's true," Harriet admitted.

"He just needs a little more training. I'll bet that if he does another dozen of these interviews he'll be a real pro."

"Let's hope not," I said, "because a dozen interviews also means a dozen crimes for which they need to ask the public for its assistance."

And then the show was over. Almost before it had begun. Gran was right. Blink and you missed it.

"That's it?" asked Scarlett. "Isn't there any more?"

"Nope, that's it," said Chase, heaving a sigh of relief. In spite of his stoic appearance clearly the burly cop had been nervous about his first television appearance.

"Are you sure?" said Marge. "Maybe there will be more after the commercial break?"

"They said they'll repeat the appeal in their late-night newsflash, and again tomorrow morning."

"Well, let's hope we get some good tips from that," said Uncle Alec.

"And let's hope this colleague has been watching," said Odelia, "and will come forward."

"It's going to be a terrible shock for the man," said Marge, "when he finds out that his colleague was murdered so soon after they met."

"Didn't Josslyn say anything about this colleague?" asked Tex.

"Only that she hadn't seen him in years, and was looking forward to catching up."

Gran now took control of the remote, and switched channels until she found one where they were playing Titanic, one of her favorite movies. The howls of protest rising up from her fellow family members quickly made her change her mind about settling in.

"Oh, all right," she grumbled, relinquishing the remote to lady of the manor Odelia. "It's not as if I don't know how it ends."

Odelia returned to the local TV station, maybe in hopes of catching some more snippets from her hubby's big interview, and for the rest of the evening, the conversation shot back and forth about a whole range of topics, hopscotching from one subject to another, as is usually the case when the members of Odelia's family get together of an evening.

"One thing's for sure," said Harriet as she placed her head on her front paws.

"What's that?" asked Brutus.

"Chase will catch this person. He's very good at catching the bad guys."

"It's not so much about catching the guy," Gran now interjected, inserting herself into our conversation and abandoning the human conversation for a moment. "It's about prevention, isn't it? I mean, if only the neighborhood watch had been out in full force last night, this crime could easily have been prevented."

The others had picked up on Gran's line of thought, and Scarlett said, "You're absolutely right, Vesta. It's simply not enough that you and me patrol our streets every night. There should be more people joining us. If only the watch consisted of a dozen or two dozen citizens, this kind of crime would be completely eradicated, and this poor woman's life would have been saved."

"You know, I usually don't agree with you," said Tex, "but for once I actually do."

"Oh, don't you start," Uncle Alec grumbled. "Keeping the streets safe and preventing crime is a job for the police, not for regular people or, God forbid, a couple of pensioners."

"So why don't you patrol those streets?" asked Gran. "Why weren't your officers patrolling that boardwalk last night? And saving Josslyn Aldridge's life?"

"We simply don't have the manpower to put a cop on every single street corner every single minute of every single day," said Uncle Alec.

Gran now turned her ire on Charlene, who, as mayor of our fair town, controls the police budget. "You have to invest more in our police force, Charlene," said the old lady. "You have to recruit and train more cops. It is what we pay taxes for, after all."

"That's fine by me," said Charlene. "If you're prepared to pay more tax, then we'll put more cops on the streets. But as long as that's not the case, I'm afraid my hands are tied."

"I have an idea," said Harriet, who'd been listening to the conversation closely. The attention of Gran, Marge and

Odelia turned to her—not coincidentally they were also the only three people who speak our language.

"What's your idea, Harriet?" asked Odelia with an indulgent smile.

"So putting cops on the streets is expensive, right?"

"Oh, it is," said Odelia. "They all need to receive a decent salary."

"And asking people to give up their leisure time to patrol the streets is a hard ask."

"Of course," said Marge. "People work all day, they have families to take care of, and what little time they have left they like to spend relaxing with their loved ones."

"There is a solution," said Harriet, and when three pairs of human eyes and three pairs of feline eyes all turned to her, she said, a sort of triumphant note in her voice: "Cats!"

"Cats?" asked Marge with a frown. "What do you mean, Harriet, sweetie?"

"So there's always plenty of cats on the streets at night, or at any other time, right?"

"Right," said Gran dubiously.

"Cats roam the streets at all hours of the day or night, and cover all of Hampton Cove. In fact that's the reason we always manage to give Odelia the kinds of tips and exclusive stories that she fills her newspaper with. So why don't we ask all the cats of Hampton Cove to form one big neighborhood watch?"

Odelia laughed. "But honey, we can't possibly expect the cats of Hampton Cove to put themselves in harm's way, just to protect the community?"

"And why not?" Harriet insisted. "Nearly all of the cats belong to somebody. And I'm sure they'd be more than happy to make sure those somebodies can feel safe in the knowledge that no one will snatch their purses and knock them dead."

Odelia, Marge and Gran now shared a look, and I could tell that Harriet's impassioned pitch had struck a chord.

"You know, Harriet?" said Odelia finally. "On second thought your idea is not so bad."

"No, and that's because it's great," said Harriet, tilting her chin a little. "And so if you make me the leader of the Neighborhood Cat Watch, I'll make sure that Hampton Cove will be the safest town on the East Coast. In fact it just might become the safest town in the whole country, and a beacon in the annals of crime fighting. And when other towns start following in our pawsteps, we'll start a revolution in crime prevention—a revolution of which we can be the proud leaders."

Gran was nodding, and so were Odelia and Marge.

"What are you guys talking about?" asked Chase, one of those rare humans who doesn't speak our language.

"Oh, nothing," Gran hastened to say.

"Why did Gran just say your idea is nothing?" asked Dooley, intrigued.

"I think she first wants to see if it's feasible," said Harriet, studying the old lady closely. "And then if it works, she can take all the credit."

"And if it fails?" asked Brutus.

"Well, since nobody knows about it except us, if it fails no one will know."

"Gran should have gone into politics," said Dooley.

"Yeah," I agreed. "She certainly has the cunning for it."

Gran now gave Harriet a wink. "Let's talk more soon," she whispered.

CHAPTER 2

The following morning, the four of us were enjoying a well-deserved nap in Odelia's office, while our human slaved away at her computer, typing up an article on the murdered woman, when all of a sudden Dan strode in, and took a seat at his star reporter's desk.

Odelia looked up with a frown. "Do you think I should talk to the friend? Get some background on Josslyn Aldridge?"

"Before you do that, I just got off the phone and I think I have an even juicier story for you, my dear."

"Oh?" said Odelia, and withdrew her hands from the keyboard. "What story?"

"How well do you know Rosa Bond?"

"Tilton Bond's wife? I've bumped into her once or twice at social events. Why?"

"It was Rosa who phoned me, and asked if she could enlist our services."

"Our services?"

Dan grinned. "And when I say 'our services' of course I

mean your services. You're really starting to make a name for yourself as an investigative reporter."

"Rosa Bond wants to hire me?"

"That's what I understood. She didn't want to talk on the phone, but I'm sure she'll tell you all about it when she arrives…" He checked his watch. "In about ten minutes."

"Rosa Bond is coming here?"

Dan nodded and got up. "I told her you'd be more than happy to place yourself at her disposal." He gave her a smile and tapped his nose. "I have a hunch this might prove to be one heck of a story." Just then, the door to the outer office opened and closed. The aged editor's pristinely white beard waggled with excitement. "I think that might be the lady already." He took a slight bow. "I'll leave you to it."

"Thanks, Dan."

"I thank you," said Dan, and quickly went to greet Mrs. Bond, or whoever it might be.

Moments later, the new arrival was ushered into Odelia's office by Dan, who quickly retreated, but not before saying, "I'll leave you in Odelia's capable hands, Mrs. Bond."

"Thanks, Mr. Goory," said the lady, and took a seat in front of Odelia.

She was a smallish woman, with short ash-blond hair and a sort of squarish face. She wasn't exactly pretty, but she had one of those kind faces, which gave the impression she was a good person at heart, and kindness always lends a certain beauty to a person, I've always thought, and this certainly was the case with Mrs. Bond.

"How old do you think she is, Max?" asked Dooley.

"Forty-something?" I said. "It's hard to say, Dooley."

"It's always hard to say with humans," my friend mused. "And I wonder why that is."

"It's because humans try to mask their real age," said Harriet. "They always want to look younger than they actually are. And so they dye their hair and apply all kinds of creams to their faces, or even have operations like facelifts or nips and tucks."

"Facelifts?" asked Dooley. "Why would you want to have your face lifted?"

"It's actually not the entire face that's lifted, Dooley," I said. "Only the parts that hang a little, like the jawline or the corners of the mouth."

"Oh, so they don't lift the whole face?"

"No, only specific sections."

He stared at the woman, who'd placed her purse on the floor and was gathering the courage to launch into her story. "But if they lift their faces, where does the part that's been lifted go? Or do they simply lift it and then trim it at the top, like a hedge?"

"Sure, Dooley," said Brutus with a grin. "They lift it and chop off the top part."

Dooley looked horrified at this. "But... what happens to the bottom part?"

"The bottom part stays where it is," said Brutus. "They grab them by the hair and simply pull from the top, see, then tie it off with a piece of twine and chop off the excess skin, and since the skin is then stretched out, the wrinkles all disappear like magic."

"But that's terrible!" said Dooley, as I could see he was picturing the gruesome procedure in vivid detail.

"And some of them do it more than once," Brutus continued, relishing in his sordid tale.

"More than once!"

"Oh, sure. They have three or four or five facelifts in a row."

"But soon there won't be any skin left!" Dooley cried.

"And that's exactly the problem with facelifts. Everything ends up in the wrong place. Their eyes are on their foreheads, their mouths are where their noses used to be, and their chins are where their mouths used to be. So they end up talking through their chin, blow their noses through their mouths and watch television from the top of their heads."

"But that's terrible!"

"Don't listen to Brutus, Dooley," I said. "He's exaggerating."

"I'm not," said Brutus with a touch of indignation, but his grin was still firmly in place, which detracted from his righteous indignation, effectively nullifying it.

"So what can I do for you, Mrs. Bond?" asked Odelia, placing her hands on her desk and interlacing her fingers.

"I find myself in something of a pickle, Mrs. Kingsley," said the woman, looking nervous as she launched into her tale.

"So you told Dan," said Odelia, nodding.

"Before we begin, I wanted to ask if I can rely on your complete discretion?"

"Absolutely," said Odelia. "Nothing of what you tell me will leave this room, unless you want it to."

The woman nodded, satisfied. "The thing is that all of a sudden I find myself the victim of… well, blackmail."

"Someone is blackmailing you?"

The woman nodded, and an expression of extreme concern slid over her face, the mask of composure slipping. "You see, before I married Tilton, I was married to another man—in fact I had a completely different life before I settled into the one I now share with my husband."

"What do you mean?"

The woman seemed to hesitate. "Promise me you won't tell anyone."

"I promise," Odelia said.

"I used to be married to a man named Clive Atcheson."

She gave Odelia an anxious look. "Maybe you've heard of him?"

"I don't think I have."

"This all happened nine years ago, in Wilmington, North Carolina, where I used to live at the time. Wilmington is where I was born, and so was Clive. You see, Clive used to run the local branch of Capital First Bank, and for a long time we were very happy. I married Clive straight out of college, and we settled down and had two kids very quickly. I was a stay-at-home mom for a while, and Clive made quite a career at the bank. We lived a good life, Mrs. Kingsley, and I can say that I was happy then. Very happy."

"So what happened?"

"Clive robbed the bank."

"He robbed his own bank?"

Mrs. Bond nodded. "One night he didn't come home, and instead two police officers showed up, and told me that Clive had taken all the money from the big vault, and had disappeared."

"My God."

"And the worst part is that his secretary also disappeared. Janice Schiller. The police told me they figured Clive and Janice were having an affair, and were in it together, and had run off with the money." She looked up, and a sad look had stolen over her face. "So you see, from one day to the next I discovered not only that my husband had been cheating on me with his secretary, but that he was a thief and that he'd robbed his bank."

"So what happened?"

She shook her head. "Later the police discovered that Clive had rented a car and had driven it across the border into Mexico. And from there the trail went cold."

"So your husband robbed the bank, then ran off to Mexico with his secretary."

"Yes. He left me with two small kids, and with a lot of questions from the police, who didn't seem to believe I wouldn't have known what he was planning. They kept a close eye on me for the next couple of months, believing that sooner or later get Clive might get in touch. Of course he never did. He's probably lying on some sandy beach somewhere, sipping cocktails and living the good life with Janice by his side. And since I found myself the subject of a lot of foul gossip, and my kids as well, I decided to leave my hometown. I changed my name from Wendy Atcheson to Rosa Gale, and we settled down here, far away from the place where I was born, and where my life had been shattered by a selfish thieving cheat. Then before long I met a man, this time a good and decent man."

"Tilton Bond."

"We hit it off, and I'm happy to say that we've been happily married for the past eight years."

"So what about this blackmailer?"

"I got a phone call last night. A male voice I didn't recognize. This man said that he knew who I was—that he knew all about my past, and if I wanted to make sure my secret didn't get out, I could buy his silence by making a generous donation. Five thousand dollars seemed like a good start, he said."

"Five thousand. That's a lot of money."

"It is, and I'm lucky enough that I can afford it. But since he said this was only the beginning, I know it won't end there. He'll just keep asking more and more. And even though my husband has money, I can't possibly ask him to hand over his entire fortune, only because he married a woman with a dark secret in her past."

"Does your husband know about your first husband and the bank robbery?"

"He does. When we met, at first I didn't want to tell him,

but the night before our wedding, I decided I couldn't go through with it unless I told him who the woman was he was about to marry." She looked up, and had tears in her eyes now. "So I said I was going to tell him something very important, and give him the opportunity to back out before it was too late. To his credit, not only didn't he back out, but he also told me that he thought I was the victim here, and had nothing to blame myself for. He also said he would have understood if I'd kept quiet about my past, but I didn't want to do that. I wanted to go into this marriage with absolute honesty as a basis to build a solid relationship. No lies."

"Did you tell him about the blackmail?"

"I did, actually."

"And what did he say?"

"He told me to go to the police. He said blackmailers will never stop asking for more and more money, especially when they see how easy it is to get it. I told him I couldn't go to the police, since the blackmailer would make sure the story of my first marriage would get out, and frankly I don't think I could face it. More importantly, I don't want my kids to face the consequences of my mistake in marrying their father."

"So what do you propose? No police?"

"Absolutely no police," said the woman adamantly.

"So you're going to pay?"

"I'm going to pay—but only this once." She gave Odelia an anxious look. "Several of my friends have told me that you are very clever and very resourceful, Mrs. Kingsley. So I was hoping that you might know of a way out of this. Without involving the police."

Odelia took a deep breath. "So you want this blackmailer to stop, but you don't want him arrested." She leaned back and thought this over.

"There must be a way to make sure my secret doesn't get

out, but also that this blackmail stops." She gave Odelia a look filled with hope.

"Frankly, in my experience blackmailers can only be stopped when the truth comes out and the secret they use as a weapon against their target is no longer a secret."

"My secret cannot come out—that's absolutely out of the question. Nobody can know that once upon a time I was Wendy Atcheson. For my children, for their future."

"How old are your kids?"

"Todd is sixteen and Aisha is fifteen. And then of course there's the baby. Alisa."

"So what age were Todd and Aisha when this happened?"

"Todd was seven and Aisha was six."

"Do they still remember their dad?"

"Yes, they do, though we hardly ever talk about him now. It just wouldn't be fair to Tilton—though I'm sure he would take it in stride. He's the most wonderful and patient man I know, and has raised Todd and Aisha as if they were his own flesh and blood—which is more than I could ever have hoped for."

"Let me think about this, Mrs. Bond. I have an idea, but I will need to discuss it with my husband first."

Mrs. Bond's face clouded. "Your husband is a police detective, isn't he?"

"He is, but I can assure you that he won't breathe a word about this to anyone."

Mrs. Bond didn't look entirely convinced, but since she didn't have a lot of options, she reluctantly agreed. "All right, but you'll have to think quick. The drop-off is arranged for tonight."

"Tonight?"

"That's right. I'm to drop off the money in the park at midnight, and make sure I'm not being followed, and that there is no police anywhere near the drop-off point."

"Which is where?"

"The playground. I'm to put the money in a plastic bag and put it in a nearby trashcan, then immediately walk away."

Odelia nodded thoughtfully. "That doesn't give us a lot of time."

"I know. I think he's doing it on purpose. Make sure I don't have time to think this through, or to set up some kind of counter… initiative."

"You know what? We'll make sure that we're ready for him."

"He said no police."

"Don't worry. He won't see us. The important thing to remember is that a blackmailer relies as much on his anonymity as he does on the secret he's got on you, and the fear he can put into you. So when we know who he is, we've already won half the battle. At that point, if we want, we can confront him."

"But won't he simply start spreading rumors about me? Or whatever evidence he has of my real identity?"

"To be honest with you, Mrs. Bond, at this point I'm as much in the dark as you are. And I think we need to play this by ear, and the first step we can take right now is to make sure we know who we're dealing with. Find out who this man is."

The woman nodded. "Of course. You're right."

"Now let's go over this again, only this time in more detail, and if you can give me your phone, and show me the number this person called you from, I think we can start to find out what we're dealing with here."

And as Mrs. Bond handed Odelia her phone, and they started making arrangements on how to handle this blackmailer, Dooley said, "I don't think she's had a facelift, Max."

"And why is that, Dooley?" I said, ruminating on Mrs. Bond's predicament.

"Can't you see? Her nose is where it should be, and so is her mouth and all the rest." He breathed a sigh of relief. "Imagine having to talk through your chin. That would be awkward, wouldn't it?"

"Yes, it most certainly would, Dooley," I said with a smile.

CHAPTER 3

After Rosa Bond had left, Odelia had gone into her editor's office, to talk the thing through. I could see from the expression on my human's face that she wasn't entirely comfortable with this latest assignment. And this is what she told Dan.

"She specifically asked me not to write about the blackmail," she said. "So frankly I don't see how this will work, Dan. I mean, she isn't paying me, and the police department isn't paying me for my time, but I still want to help. So how do we do this?"

"I'll pay you for your time," said Dan.

"But didn't you hear what I just said? I won't be able to use any of it for the paper. So what's the point?"

"The point is that you will be helping a woman in need. And that's all that matters."

"But—"

"She can't go to the police?"

"No. She doesn't want to expose her kids to what happened nine years ago."

Dan shrugged. "So you help her. And so what if we can't

use it for the paper? Sometimes we simply want to help people, Odelia. Because it's the right thing to do."

"But, Dan…"

"Do you think I haven't hunted down stories and not been able to use any of it in the end—simply because people asked me not to print it? Of course I have!"

"I see."

"Look, we're reporters, and we're in the business of looking for great stories. But because of our very specific skillset sometimes we're able to do what the police can't. And that's fine. In fact that's great." He gave her an encouraging smile. "Now go out there and make an old man proud. Catch this blackmailer and make sure he never blackmails again."

"You're a very peculiar editor, Dan, has anyone ever told you that?"

"Oh, many people," said the newspaperman with a grin. "I consider it a compliment."

And as Odelia got on the phone to confer with her husband on how best to handle this situation that had cropped up, I decided to do a little digging into Rosa Bond's past. Frankly I was intrigued, and curious to find out if the story had indeed played out the way she described it.

So I settled down with the tablet Odelia bought for us. Harriet and Brutus had left the office to take a little stroll and stretch their legs, so it was just Dooley and me.

It didn't take long for us to hit on several news stories describing the events as they'd transpired nine years ago in the fair city of Wilmington, North Carolina. Rosa's name had indeed been Wendy Atcheson back then, happily married to Clive Atcheson, branch manager of the Capital First Bank. Until the day the man had absconded with the entire contents of his vault, and subsequently run off to Mexico with his secretary Janice Schiller. The total haul of the criminal couple had been a cool five million. Not a bad sum if you wanted to live the good life down South, where cost of living is modest, and it's easy to fly under the radar with your illegally acquired nest egg. The fact that he had to leave his wife and kids behind didn't seem to have bothered the banker too much, for he'd never been seen or heard from since, and even though the case had never been officially closed, and he was still a wanted man there hadn't been a new development for the past nine years.

"Look at this picture, Dooley," I said, zooming in on a picture of what looked like a company Christmas party.

"Oh, look, that's Rosa Bond," said Dooley, pointing to a woman who stood with raised champagne flute in the foreground. Next to her was a man who was, according to the caption, the banker-slash-robber himself: Clive Atcheson. They were both smiling at the camera, snazzily dressed and clearly having a great time.

"They look so happy," said Dooley.

"When was this picture taken?" I asked, studying the rest of the article in which the photo had been featured. "Ten years ago. This must have been the Christmas just before it happened."

"Their last Christmas," said Dooley. "Isn't that a song?"

"I think it is," I said, though I wasn't all that interested in cultural references. I wanted to find out if the secretary was also in the picture, which would have been an interesting find. I studied the caption, where a few names were mentioned. The picture had appeared in the society section of the Wilmington Times. And then I found her. Janice Schiller. A russet-haired voluptuous woman, standing right behind her boss, and looking in his direction with a gleam of what could only be interpreted as smoldering passion in her eyes.

"Oh, she loved him, Max," said Dooley. "Just look at the way she's looking at him."

"Indeed she did, Dooley," I agreed. "She loved him with a passion."

"Bonnie and Clyde, they were."

"Well, not exactly," I said. "Bonnie and Clyde left a trail of death and destruction in their wake. These two simply disappeared the moment they crossed the border."

I studied the picture some more, and noticed a man looking in Janice's direction with a sort of wistful look on his face. He was a man with receding hairline and a weak chin, no doubt one of many of Janice's male admirers. Clearly the woman had been some kind of local femme fatale, twisting men around her little finger without any problem.

"Poor Rosa," said Dooley. "Having to leave her old life behind, just because her husband decided to become a fugitive from justice."

"Yeah, and think about those poor kids. Todd and Aisha not only lost their dad, but all of their friends—their entire life, in fact."

"I'm glad that Odelia decided to help them," said Dooley. "And I hope she catches this blackmailer in the act and makes him stop."

"Yeah, let's hope she does," I agreed. "For Rosa's sake, and her family." Hampton Cove is a bucolic little town, but gossip can be fierce and vicious, even in a wonderful community like ours, and Rosa wouldn't be the first person driven away by the wagging tongues of a few gossipmongers.

"I think this family deserves a break," said Dooley.

And never truer words were spoken.

CHAPTER 4

We decided to get a little air ourselves, while Odelia made the necessary arrangements for tonight. Cats don't like to be cooped up inside for too long. We don't need to be walked like dogs, since we can very well walk ourselves, thank you very much, but we still like to get out and about at regular intervals. And so as we passed out onto the street, we soon came upon Gran and Scarlett, who were seated in their usual spot, in the Star Hotel's outside dining area, sipping from their beverages, and conversing with Harriet and Brutus, who'd jumped up on a chair and were taking in a bit of sunshine.

Dooley and I decided to occupy the remaining chair, and enjoy some company while also engaging in one of our favorite activities that we share with the two older ladies: people watching. Main Street spread out before us, and since the heart of town is where all the activity is concentrated, we never stint for something interesting to see there.

"I think it's a great idea, Harriet," Gran was saying, "but I've been doing some thinking, and I think I've come up with a very important improvement on your original setup."

"What improvement?" asked Harriet suspiciously. It was obvious she didn't feel her brilliant ideas could be improved upon.

"What are you talking about, Gran?" asked Dooley.

"You remember how Harriet suggested we launch a neighborhood cat watch?"

"Oh, of course," said Dooley. "That's going to be a lot of fun, isn't it?"

"I'm sure it will be. Only problem is: how to organize all that information—or like those Silicon Valley whizz kids like to call it: how to handle all that data!"

"What data?" asked Scarlett, who had a hard time following the flow of words between Gran and her cats. Like Chase, she doesn't have that special gift that enables her to converse with us.

"Okay, so let's assume that there are always a dozen cats on every street, and every cat sends back information about what they see to the neighborhood watch. With me so far?"

"Uh-huh," said Scarlett, taking a sip from her cappuccino.

"Now multiply that by the number of streets in this town. Which is..." She frowned, then, since she couldn't be bothered, concluded, "a lot. A whole lot of data!"

"Too much, if you ask me."

"I agree. So we need to up our game and come up with a solution. And that solution is... an app!" said Gran with an air of 'ta-dah!'

"An app," said Scarlett with a frown.

"An app! Apps are all the rage, hon!"

"I know they're all the rage, but we don't know the first thing about app development. In fact sometimes I have a hard time using the apps on my phone."

"And that's where Kevin comes in."

"Kevin? As in my grandnephew Kevin?"

"Exactly! He's the computer nerd in the family, right?"

"Uh-huh."

"So? He can build us an app that can talk to this database... thingie."

"I guess so. But I still don't see..."

"That's because I haven't told you the best part yet."

"Which is?"

"We develop an app and we give it some cool name. Like iCat or whatever. Some name that is easy to remember. And once we have it—we promote the hell out of it, and bingo!"

"Bingo?"

"We sell it to one of the big boys and become millionaires!"

"You lost me again, hon."

Gran sighed, like one who has to contend with lesser minds than her own. Einstein probably had to deal with this kind of thing all the time. "Okay, so cats spy for us, see?"

"I'm with you so far."

"Hundreds of cats, or even thousands. Covering the entire Hampton Cove territory. There won't be an inch of this town we won't be able to monitor through their eyes."

"Uh-huh."

"Now all of those cats will be equipped with smart collars—audio and video included—sending their data back to a database where it's all collected and analyzed and sent to our app, courtesy of Kevin."

"Oh... kay," said Scarlett, sounding dubious about her grandnephew's capacity to build such an amazing app, but still prepared to give the plan the benefit of the doubt.

"So then the system automatically comes up with the threats that need to be addressed: burglaries in progress, domestic disputes, drunks tearing up the neighborhood, vandals spraying graffiti on town hall... what have you."

"Car thieves breaking into cars, jealous men keying their

neighbors' new Jaguar," said Scarlett, getting the gist of the thing.

"Exactly! And that information is then automatically sent to us, and either we go after the criminals, or we liaise with the police and they send a couple of officers to deal with the crime, while it is *still in progress*," she said, stressing this last part by pounding the table with a bony fist, making her hot chocolate drink and Scarlett's cappuccino jump merrily up and down to the beat of Gran's pretty excitement.

"That all sounds wonderful," said Scarlett. "But I'm not sure how feasible it is."

"It's perfectly feasible. On one condition and one condition only."

"And what is that?"

"That the people handling the data are well-versed in the feline language. I mean, how else are they going to be able to interpret what all of those thousands of cats are saying?"

"Oh," said Scarlett, and her face sagged.

"What?"

"You know I can't talk cat, honey."

"Yes, I know that, but there's no reason why you can't learn."

Scarlett frowned. "You mean…"

"Exactly! With my help, and the assistance of my four precious darlings here, I'm sure you'll be able to pick up the language in no time. And then it's simply a matter of taking turns manning GHQ and coordinating the whole thing."

"Oh, I would love to learn their language," said Scarlett, giving me a pat on the head, which I responded to by giving her a soft purr in return. I like Scarlett, always have, even when she and Gran were archenemies and fought tooth and nail at every opportunity.

"I'll teach her, Gran," said Harriet. "After all, this was my idea in the first place."

"I know it was your idea, Harriet," said Gran, giving the prissy Persian a tickle under her chin. "And definitely one of your better ones."

"You really think so?"

"Of course! We could wipe out crime in the whole country if we get this thing rolling."

"Wouldn't that be nice," said Dooley. "No more crime anywhere."

"It would also mean that there wouldn't be cops anymore," Brutus pointed out, "which would mean that Chase and Uncle Alec would be out of a job."

"I doubt it," said Harriet. "There will still have to be cops to respond to the tips they receive from the Neighborhood Cat Watch."

"Yeah, I guess you're right," Brutus admitted.

"Crime will only disappear as long as we remain vigilant, sugar pants. Those criminals will always be criminals, and they'll still want to engage in their acts of criminal activity. It's us who will stand in their way, and so vigilance is key." She turned to Gran. "Did you mention something about us becoming millionaires, Gran?"

"Well, as soon as the app is working the way it should, we'll get a lot of attention. And you know what that means, right?"

"That... I'll need to have new pictures taken?"

"That the big boys will fall over each other to buy us out! Google, Microsoft, Facebook—they'll stand in line with their checkbooks, offering us millions for the app. There will be a bidding war, because let's face it—who doesn't want to get rid of crime? In fact it wouldn't surprise me, when the dust settles, that we'll make a hundred million dollars."

"A hundred million dollars!" Harriet cried.

"At the very least!"

"How many nuggets of kibble is that?" asked Brutus.

I could already see the dollar signs flashing in Harriet's eyes, and even though I could have told her there were major flaws in Gran's plan, I knew she wouldn't be susceptible to my counter-arguments, so I wisely conserved my energy and kept my tongue.

"Okay, but so first things first," said Gran. "Scarlett, you need to talk to Kevin, and tell him to start working on that app. Also, you need to sit down with Harriet and start learning the language."

"Oh, goodie," said Scarlett, as she high-fived Harriet at this point. Okay, so maybe it was a low-five. Cats are, after all, vertically challenged when compared with humans.

And since it seemed clear that our presence was no longer required, Dooley and I took our leave. Harriet might be getting ready to become a multimillionaire, but we had a blackmailer to catch, and frankly that seemed more important than Gran's elusive app.

CHAPTER 5

"Do you think that Scarlett will be able to learn our language, Max?" asked Dooley.

"Somehow I doubt it, Dooley," I said.

"Why? Don't you think she's clever enough?"

"Oh, I think she's certainly clever enough, but my impression has always been that being able to talk to cats is a gift, not something that can be taught." A gift passed along the female line, otherwise Uncle Alec would have been able to talk to us as well.

"So that means that Gran and Harriet's plan is a bust?"

"Not necessarily. It is true that if you outfit a cat with a camera and a microphone, they'll be able to pick up certain things, but unless they're trained to pay attention to criminal activity, what they'll pick up is simply the kinds of things cats are naturally interested in: what birds are tootling in the trees, or a piece of fish filet someone left on the windowsill to cool off. And those things aren't necessarily indicative of a crime."

"If the cat steals the fish filet it is a crime," said Dooley.

I smiled. "Yeah, but I don't think it's the kind of crime that will make Gran a multimillionaire."

We'd arrived at the General Store, where our friend Kingman likes to hold forth in front of the store. His human Wilbur was behind the counter as usual, scanning the wares as they passed him by on the conveyor belt, meanwhile keeping an eye on the television screen, where an old black-and-white episode of Zorro was playing.

"Hey, you guys," said Kingman when we came trudging up. "How are things in the world of crime?"

"Not too good," I said. "A woman just walked into Odelia's office hoping to get rid of a blackmailer."

"A blackmailer, huh?" said Kingman. "Nasty business, blackmail."

"Yeah, especially since a blackmailer never stops, unless the big secret is out in the open, and that's exactly what this woman can't afford."

"So who's the woman, and what is her secret?"

And so in a few short words I told him the story as Rosa had conveyed it to Odelia.

"Five million bucks. I can understand why she wants to keep it a secret. Though if I'm being totally honest, my suggestion would be to stop worrying about the secret, and catch that blackmailer before he makes any more victims."

"But what about her future? And the future of her kids?"

"Look, her husband already knows, so from that side she will get all the support she needs. And the kids are nine years older now, and probably not as vulnerable as they used to be. And frankly I don't think people will care that much. It's all ancient history now. And also, it didn't happen here, and you know how people don't care a hoot about what happens elsewhere. And thirdly, she didn't do anything wrong, if I understood you correctly. It's the ex-husband who committed a crime, so why should she and her kids suffer?"

"Good points," I said, nodding. "I hadn't thought of it that way."

"I think if people found out what this woman went through, they'd show her compassion and support instead of scorn and suspicion. Just my two cents."

"No, but you're absolutely right."

"Do you think cats can get a facelift, Kingman?" asked Dooley now.

Kingman frowned. "What do cats need facelifts for?"

"Well, when their jawlines starts to sag," said Dooley. "To lift them, you know."

"Look, Dooley, we have one advantage over humans: our faces are covered with fur. So if we get a sagging jawline or the odd wrinkle, who cares? No one will notice."

Dooley thought about this for a moment, then said, "But then why don't humans simply let their beards grow out? That way they can cover their faces with fur, too."

"Oh, but they do," said Kingman. "Haven't you noticed that when men get older, they suddenly decide to grow a beard? It's simply so they can hide that sagging jawline under an inch of fuzz."

"So why don't women do the same thing?"

"Because women don't grow beards, Dooley."

"But they do," said Dooley. "Gran has a mustache, but she waxes it. I've seen her do it. I've asked her why, but she won't say. She just said she doesn't want to look like a Yeti."

Both Kingman and I laughed heartily at this, but since Dooley kept staring at us, clearly expecting an answer to his unasked question, I finally said, "Look, Dooley. Bearded women aren't as universally accepted as bearded men."

"But why not?"

"Because humans like to adhere to certain standards of beauty, and a woman with a beard simply doesn't fit into that concept."

"Well, it should," said Dooley. "It would solve all of their problems. They could hide their jawlines when they sag and they could also hide the wrinkles around their mouths."

"Great," I said. "You tell Gran, and maybe she can start spreading the word."

"Oh, but I will, Max," said Dooley. "I think it's a lot less painful than pulling up your face and then chopping off the excess skin. Or ripping out those hairs with hot wax."

"What excess skin?" asked Kingman, clearly at a loss.

"Didn't you know, Kingman? People have their faces lifted and the excess skin surgically removed." His eyes went wide. "That's probably why people lose their hair when they're older: it's simply chopped off at the top, along with all that wrinkly skin!"

"You just might be right, Dooley," said Kingman, as he glanced over to his human. I followed his gaze, and saw how Wilbur was indeed getting thinner on top, and how the beard he'd started growing had moved up his face. It used to start around his Adam's apple but now started just below his chin, and had almost reached his eyes.

"Soon his eyebrows will be on top of his head," said Dooley in hushed tones, "and his beard will cover the place where his eyes used to be. He'll have to part the hairs to see."

I shivered, and I think we all praised a benevolent god who'd made sure that cats never had to go through the terrible ordeal of the so-called facelift.

And as we said goodbye to Kingman, he reminded us to talk to Odelia, and to tell Rosa not to be afraid to confront her blackmailer. She would be just fine if he told the whole world about her secret, and I can't say I didn't think Kingman was right on the money.

CHAPTER 6

That night, a veritable welcoming committee was awaiting the blackmailer and lying in wait for his arrival. The particular trashcan the blackmailer had told Rosa Bond to dump the bag of money in was located directly underneath a lamppost… which was out of order.

"I think he must have picked this spot for this exact reason," said Chase, who was located in the bushes directly opposite the trashcan, along with Odelia. "Which means he thought this out in advance."

"I still think we should have asked Uncle Alec to dispatch a couple of his officers," said Odelia. "What if he manages to escape?"

"No way," said Chase. "He'll have to run really fast if he wants to beat me."

"Chase sounds very confident, Max," said Dooley. "Do you really think he will be able to catch the blackmailer?"

"I'm sure he will, Dooley," I said. "Chase is very fit."

"Chase *is* very fit," Dooley admitted.

We gave the man a look of admiration. Chase looked in

fine fettle tonight, and even seemed eager to confront Rosa's blackmailer.

"That's why he's such a great cop," said Dooley.

"Because he's so fit?"

"Because he's never afraid to confront the bad guys."

Just then, a lone figure came wandering along the path. Rosa didn't look left or right, but immediately dumped a small plastic bag into the trashcan, placed there by the town council for the purpose of receiving cigarette butts, candy wrappers, chewing gum, dog excrement, but most definitely not five thousand dollars wrapped in one of the General Store's generic plastic baggies. Then again, humans have always been very creative in thinking up ways to repurpose household objects like plastic bags. Nowadays they turn them into park benches, backyard decks and fences and even playground equipment. So this particular plastic bag might one day make its way back to the park—minus the cash.

Rosa quickly walked on, as she'd been instructed to, and now the long wait began for the crook who'd forced her to pay up to avoid her past becoming common knowledge.

And we didn't have to wait long: suddenly a man came trudging up that same path, looked left and right, then dipped into the trash receptacle, took out the plastic bag, and then tucked it into his coat and was off at a nice clip! All in all a very smooth operator!

"Let's grab him!" Chase said, and was out of those bushes and proving his parents correct in naming him Chase: he hurried in the direction of the blackmailer, and made haste doing so. Unfortunately the blackmailer must have seen him coming, for he, too, quickened his step, then broke into an outright run. Odelia had sprang from the bushes like a coiled spring, and even Dooley and myself were giving chase, though at a much more sedate tempo. And as the chase was on, we could see Chase gaining on the blackmailer, and I anticipated an imminent capture any moment when all of a sudden, out of the bushes Gran and Scarlett appeared, followed by Harriet and Brutus. They crossed Chase's path as the cop was in the homestretch to tackle the blackmailer, and their timing was thus that Gran collided with Chase, Scarlett collided with Odelia, Harriet collided with Dooley, and Brutus collided with me. So on the whole you might say that it was one serendipitous collision, and the upshot was that by the time all the limbs had been disentangled, and all the heads had been screwed on right again, and the loud and vociferous recriminations had died away, of our blackmailer there was not a single trace.

In other words, the neighborhood watch—or should I call them the Neighborhood Cat Watch now?—had effectively been instrumental in allowing the bad guy to get away.

Not a propitious start for Gran and Harriet's latest harebrained scheme!

The conversation that followed wasn't a very fruitful one, either.

"You let him get away!" Chase cried.

"Let who get away?" asked Gran, massaging a sore spot where the large and muscular cop had bumped into her. It was in fact a small miracle that all her body parts were still attached and that she was still breathing. If a man of Chase's dimensions had bumped into me, going at that speed, I would have been flattened. Like running into a bulldozer.

"Can't tell you," Chase grunted, scanning the horizon for the elusive blackmailer.

"Can't tell me what?"

"Sorry—it's classified," the cop announced.

"Classified? Who are you? James Bond? Do you have a license to kill, too? Cause you tried to kill me just now!"

"As if," Chase scoffed. He was clearly annoyed that he'd lost his man.

"Chase is probably right," said Dooley. "I think Gran is very hard to kill."

"Oh, don't say things like that, Dooley," said Harriet. "It's upsetting."

"No, but it's true. She reminds me of a certain bug."

"What bug?" asked Harriet.

"Well, it was in a Discovery Channel documentary the other night. There's this bug that can survive anything. They've even shot it into space and it survived. Now what are they called?"

"Tartigrades," I said. I'd also seen this particular documentary.

"That's it!" Dooley cried.

"Also called water bears or moss piglets."

"Who are you calling a moss piglet?" asked Gran, giving me a dangerous look.

"So who were you chasing?" asked Brutus, getting back to the point at issue.

"Oh, you know, Brutus," I said. "You were in Odelia's office this morning."

"Oh, that," said Brutus, as if suddenly remembering what was the most important case that had come our way in weeks.

"Who were they chasing, Brutus?" asked Gran.

"Umm…" said Brutus, cutting a quick glance to Odelia, who placed a finger to her lips in the universal sign of 'Shut up if you know what's good for you!' And so Brutus did shut up, because he did know what was good for him—and who.

"Oh, don't be like that," said Gran. "We're all part of the same neighborhood watch now. And us neighborhood watchers don't keep secrets from each other. That's immoral."

"Immoral!" spat Chase. "Wanna know what's immoral? Sabotaging our operation!"

"If only you'd told us about your 'operation,' Mr. Bond, we could have helped you!" said Gran, getting a little hot under her collar.

Dooley uttered a giggle, causing all eyes to turn to him. "Mr. Bond," he said. "It's funny, because we're working for Mrs. Bond."

"Mrs. Bond? Who's Mrs. Bond?" said Gran.

"Rosa Bond?" asked Scarlett. "The wife of Tilton Bond?"

"Who's Tilton Bond?" asked Gran. "James Bond's brother?"

"He used to run an internet business, then sold it for a lot of money and since then he's set up a foundation and has been giving a lot of his money to charity."

"Nutjob," Gran grunted. Clearly she couldn't understand why anyone would give their precious millions to charity.

Odelia turned to her husband. "Maybe we better tell her," she said.

"I thought your client had sworn you to absolute secrecy?"

"Yeah, but Gran won't tell anyone, will you, Gran?"

"Me? Tell anyone? Never has there ever been anyone as discreet as me."

Scarlett made a scoffing sound at that, but when Gran gave her a look that could kill, she quickly shut up.

"Look, this has to remain between the four of us, all right?" said Odelia.

"Absolutely—now spill."

And so Odelia proceeded to explain to her grandmother and Scarlett the circumstances of our nocturnal stakeout. It caused the two friends to utter a whistle of surprise.

"Five million dollars," said Scarlett. "No wonder she had to change her name and move out here to the sticks."

"Why?" asked Odelia.

"Honey, whenever that kind of money is involved, all

kinds of vermin comes crawling out of the woodwork wanting a piece of it. Just look at this blackmailer. I'm sure there will be others just like him. In fact it's a small miracle she's been able to keep this a secret for so long. People are bound to find out, and if you think like a criminal, you probably figure that Rosa Bond is still in touch with the father of her kids, and if she is, why not give an enterprising crook his coordinates in Mexico, so they can organize a 'rescue party.' Rescue what's left of that five million dollars, not the man himself—who'll probably find himself on the operative side of a deadly gun and then in a shallow grave—him and his secretary."

I turned to Dooley. "So maybe Kingman was wrong to figure it would be best to share Rosa's secret with the world."

"Yeah, he probably was," my friend agreed.

"What was Kingman's advice?" asked Odelia, curious.

"Well, he figured that since Rosa didn't do anything wrong, people would be sympathetic if they found out about what happened."

"He's got a point," said Gran. "Except that Scarlett also has a point. That kind of money brings out the worst in people, and so maybe it's best if nobody finds out." She smiled at her friend. "Now tell me, honey. How much of this conversation have you picked up?"

"To be honest? Not one iota."

"Not a single word?"

"Not a thing."

"Don't worry, Scarlett," said Chase. "I don't understand them either and that's fine. Lucky for me I've got my sweetheart to translate for me."

"Yeah, but it's very important that I learn their language," said Scarlett.

"Important why?" asked Odelia.

"Um…" Scarlett looked to Gran, who shook her head decidedly.

"I'm sorry," said the old lady. "I'm afraid it's a secret."

"A secret!" Odelia cried. "But I just told you my secret!"

"Yeah, well, that's where you and I are different: you can't keep a secret, but I can. Now let's skedaddle, Scarlett."

"Where are you going?" asked Chase.

"Scarlett is going to attend cat choir, and see if she can't pick up a few words."

And before Odelia had recovered from her indignation, the two friends had indeed skedaddled, and so had Brutus and Harriet.

And since cat choir is indeed a very important social event, Dooley and I took our leave as well.

I mean, why stick around? That blackmailer was probably on the other side of town by now, counting his money and thanking his lucky stars.

And wondering how much he was going to ask the next time.

Ten thousand? Twenty? Thirty?

Easy pickings.

CHAPTER 7

The next morning I woke up from a peaceful slumber, lying at the foot of my human's bed, and yawned and stretched, as one does, when I noticed a pair of eyes fixed on me. I gave the starer a kindly smile. "Hey, Brutus. Sleep well?"

"Are you sure you're all right, Max?" my friend said.

"Um, yeah, I think so," I said. Of course one never really knows if one is all right, does one? I mean, there can be any number of things wrong with you and you'll never know. The feline body is, after all, a complex machine, and difficult even for its inhabitant to fully fathom. But I had a feeling Brutus wasn't interested in these philosophical ruminations, so I didn't go into all that. Instead, I said, "Why? Do you think something is wrong with me?" Oftentimes it's the outsider who can see things you as the so-called insider cannot.

"Just that when you ran into me last night you may have sustained permanent damage. Then again, the effect might be delayed, of course."

"What effect?" I asked, now thoroughly bewildered. "What permanent damage?"

"Are you permanently damaged, Max?" asked Dooley, who'd also woken up now and was following the conversation with rising concern.

"It's just that when you run into a muscular cat like me, it's almost like running into a brick wall," Brutus explained. "And the damage, if not immediate, could manifest later on."

"You mean like when Road Runner falls off a cliff and only breaks up into a thousand little pieces after there's been a delay for comedic purposes?" said Dooley, who's big on the Cartoon Network, at least when he's not diligently watching the Discovery Channel.

"Something like that," Brutus allowed. He was still regarding me with marked concern. "Watch my paw, Max, can you do that for me? Just your eyeballs—keep your head still." And to demonstrate what he meant, he moved his paw in front of my face from the left to the right and back again. I followed his paw eagerly, without moving my head.

"How am I doing?" I asked finally.

"Mh," said Brutus. "Everything seems to be in order. Though to be absolutely sure you probably need to see a neurologist. They can do some more extensive testing to see if you didn't suffer any brain damage."

"Brain damage!" Dooley cried. "Max, do you think you have brain damage?"

"I don't think so," I said, and shook my head a little, just to make sure my brain was still present and accounted for. "I don't have a headache, if that's what you mean," I said.

"Yeah, a headache would be a clear indication that your brain is all shook up," Brutus agreed.

Harriet now also woke up and stretched languorously before opening her eyes and taking in the scene. "What's going on?" she asked. "Why are you all looking as if somebody died?"

"Brutus thinks Max has brain damage from running into him last night," said Dooley.

"It's like running into a brick wall, see," said Brutus, reiterating his earlier point. "And I have to say I take full responsibility, Max. When you have the kind of otherworldly physicality I have, your body turns into a lethal weapon, even if you don't mean it to."

"Oh, pookie bear, Max didn't run into you that hard," said Harriet.

"Yeah, you probably have a point," said Brutus. "Max is big and sluggish, so he probably isn't capable of reaching the kind of speed required to do serious damage when suddenly brought to a stop by hitting an unyielding rocklike object like myself." He clapped me on the shoulder, almost making me topple off the bed. "I'm sure you'll be just fine, Max," he said, giving me the smile a doctor would give a cancer patient who he knows only has a couple of weeks to live and doesn't want to worry.

"But... I did hit you pretty hard last night, Brutus," I said.

"Yeah, but like Harriet pointed out, you weren't going that fast, Max, so I'm sure everything is fine up there underneath that ivory dome of yours." And to show us he meant what he said, he gave me a hard rap on the noggin.

"Ouch," I murmured. "I felt that."

"I'm sorry, Max," he said, immediately rueful. "I guess I don't know my own strength." He sighed. "That's the problem when you're as strong and muscular as I am: you end up hurting your friends and loved ones, even though you simply can't help it. The Rock must have the same problem. And Superman, of course."

"I bumped into Harriet last night," said Dooley. "Do you think I have brain damage, too?"

Brutus smiled at this. "You need to have a brain before it can get damaged, Dooley."

"Don't be mean, snuggle bunny," said Harriet as she yawned once again.

"I'm not being mean. I'm just pointing out a physical fact: when you don't have a brain, it can't get damaged." He gave up another wistful sigh. "I wish sometimes that I was like Dooley. As it is, I simply can't stop thinking—can't turn off the old noodle, you know. Keep thinking about the new mission."

"What mission?" I asked, giving our humans a keen glance, wondering when they would get up.

"Well, we talked things through last night, while you guys were chasing that blackmailer—unsuccessfully, I might add—and we've come up with a sound plan of campaign."

"Is that so?" I said, not all that interested in Brutus's plan.

"Yeah, Harriet is going to teach Scarlett to talk to cats, while I start recruiting the Baker Street Cats."

"Baker Street what?"

"You remember the Baker Street Boys, right?"

"Oh, sure," I said. "Sherlock Holmes's youthful helpers."

"Who are the Baker Street Boys, Max?" asked Dooley.

"Well, Sherlock Holmes had a group of youthful street urchins who helped him tackle his cases and solve crimes. They'd spy the streets of London and report back to him."

"Homeless kids, mostly," said Brutus. "Living rough on London's mean streets. They were called the Baker Street Boys because that's where Holmes lived: in Baker Street. And that's what gave me the idea—"

"What gave me the idea," Harriet interjected.

"What gave us the idea. Neighborhood Cat Watch sounds so boring, and Baker Street Cats has a nice ring to it, don't you think?"

"Shouldn't it be Harrington Street Cats, since we live in Harrington Street?" asked Dooley.

Brutus decided to ignore him and went on, "So like the

Baker Street Boys reported back to Sherlock Holmes, our Baker Street Cats will report to their own brilliant detective: me."

"You mean me, snickerdoodle," said Harriet.

"We're still working out the details," said Brutus.

"Uh-huh," I said.

"So I'll be teaching the human operators to talk to cats," said Harriet, "and Brutus will train a network of cats to patrol the streets of Hampton Cove and bring us anything that might tell us that a crime is being committed or planned. Isn't that just great?"

It certainly sounded like a plan, I thought. "And how are all those cats going to communicate with you?" I asked.

"Well, Gran wanted us all to wear our smart collars again, but I put my paw down and said no."

"We told her we hate those smart collars," said Brutus.

He wasn't lying. Twice now our humans had tried to outfit us with collars—first the usual kind, and the second time around some snazzy high-tech collars with GPS tracking and the capacity to monitor our vital signs. In both cases the conclusion had been that cats and collars don't mix, and I was glad the plan had been nipped in the bud this time.

"I'll go out there and talk to my lieutenants," said Brutus, "and those lieutenants will talk to the soldiers, and so on down to the lowest echelon. I'm not going to bother you with the details, but it's a complicated but highly effective structure. Like an army."

"So you're building yourself an army now, are you?" I said.

"Yeah, an army of cats, designed to keep our streets safe." He thrust out his chest. "I think it's going to be the greatest thing since sliced bread, and Gran thinks so, too. And when all is said and done, and we're fully operational, Gran will get in touch with potential investors, and we'll roll out the Baker

Street Cats project to neighboring towns, then to the entire county, the state, the country, and finally the whole world."

"Global domination," I murmured. "Very James Bond."

"I know, right?" said Brutus, glowing with pride.

"There are cats everywhere," said Harriet, pointing out the obvious. "There are cats in China, in Japan, in the Middle-East, in Africa, and even in faraway places like Europe. So there's no reason the Baker Street Cats app we're building won't be a big hit all over the world." She grinned at her mate, who gave her an affectionate grin in return, and they shared a smooch. "It's going to be grand, snuggle pooh. Just grand."

"I know it is, sugar britches," said Brutus.

Boy, was I glad not having to be a part of this new global army of cats.

"So how about it, Max?" said Brutus.

"How about what?" I asked.

"I need a second-in-command. A loyal lieutenant who I can trust implicitly, and who will carry out my orders unflinchingly and without asking questions. You up for the task?"

"No, thank you, Brutus," I said. "I'll pass."

He frowned. "What do you mean, you'll pass? Don't you want the streets of Hampton Cove to be free from crime?"

"Oh, absolutely, but I'm not sure this is the way to do it."

"What are you talking about? This is a fool-proof plan. In fact it's the only plan."

I gave him a gentle pat on the back. "And I'm sure you're the right cat for the job, Brutus. But frankly I have other things to do."

"What other things?!"

"Yeah, Max," Harriet chimed in. "What could possibly be more important than the Baker Street Cats?"

"Protecting Rosa Bond from her blackmailer, for one

thing," I said. "And making sure she gets her five thousand dollars back."

Brutus made a throwaway gesture with his paw. "That's peanuts, Max. I'm talking major crime prevention here. We're going after the big guns. The people that are laying waste to our community, preying on the innocent and destroying the social fabric of this town."

"Well, I think catching Rosa's blackmailer is a good start," I said.

Brutus gave me a nasty look. "I think you hit your head harder than you thought last night, cause this kind of thinking is indicative of some major brain damage right there."

"Oh, no," said Dooley, slapping a paw to his mouth. "Max, you have to get an MIR as soon as possible!"

"You mean an MRI?"

"That one, too."

Just then, the doorbell chimed, and I was glad, for it saved me from having to contend with Brutus's cat army, and Dooley's concern for my apparently very feeble brain.

Odelia stirred, and so did Chase, but it took another couple of attempts by our unknown visitor to finally wake them sufficiently to crawl from underneath the covers and head down the stairs to open the door.

"Oh, it's you," said Odelia without much enthusiasm. And when I arrived downstairs to see who this could possibly be, I saw it was none other than Uncle Alec.

"I'm afraid there's been a murder," said the Chief as he took in his frumpy-looking niece.

Chase, also stomping down the stairs, and looking much too refreshed for a man who'd only turned in late last night, frowned and said, "A murder? What do you mean?"

Uncle Alec sniffed the air. "Is that coffee I smell?"

The hint was obvious, and while a sleepy-looking Odelia

popped a capsule into the coffeemaker, Chase had already popped back upstairs and moments later we heard the shower running.

Brutus might be built like a brick wall, but so was his human, and all that brick needed regular maintenance to keep it in excellent shape. And while Uncle Alec took a seat at the kitchen counter, and proceeded to inform his niece about this most recent crime, the rest of the cat contingent made their way down, and I told Brutus, "There's been a murder. Time to instruct your lieutenants and your soldiers to start looking for clues and such."

But Brutus held up his paw. "I'm afraid I don't have time to deal with that right now, Max. You'll have to handle this one on your own, I'm afraid."

"Oh? But I thought—"

He shook his head. "You don't understand what an enormous undertaking the Baker Street Cats is, do you, Max? First we need to put an entire infrastructure in place. There's meetings we need to conduct, people that need to be trained, an organization that needs to be built. It will take time before we're fully operational. But once we are, you better watch out, for here we come."

But instead of coming, he was going, disappearing through the cat flap.

I glanced up to Odelia. "Is it all right if Dooley and I tag along, Odelia?"

"Oh, absolutely," she said, having trouble keeping her eyes open. That's what you get when you spend half the night trying to catch a blackmailer: you look like a train wreck in the morning. And since Odelia has never been a morning person to begin with…

Chase now came thundering down the stairs, looking like the Energizer Bunny.

"Tell me all, buddy!" he yelled, causing Odelia to wince

and shake her head.

CHAPTER 8

Turns out the victim of this latest crime had come to a sticky end in our very own street. And so two Harrington Street Cats—me and Dooley—found ourselves a couple of houses down from the one we call home, and staring at the body of the recently deceased.

The house itself was of the dilapidated kind, and not nearly as nice as most of the houses on the block. Then again, once upon a time probably all the houses had been like this: a little cramped and not exactly up to modern specs. But over the years houses had been torn down and rebuilt, and others renovated. Willie Dornhauser's house had escaped this remodeling craze, and I would like to say that it had stood the test of time but unfortunately that wasn't the case. Mr. Dornhauser, too, looked a little dilapidated, and I'm not saying this merely because he was dead. His hair was unkempt, and so were his clothes, and he had a ratty sort of facial growth on his chin and a ruddy face, now slightly less ruddy, presumably, than when he'd still been amongst the living.

Abe Cornwall, the county coroner, sat crouched next to

the dead man, examining him closely, as a country coroner does, then finally shook his head. "He's dead," he announced in a mournful baritone.

"I know he's dead, Abe," said Chase. "But what made him this way, that's what I would like to know."

"Well, that's fairly obvious, isn't it?" said the heavyset coroner as he got up with some effort and some serious cracking sounds coming from both knees. He pointed to a sort of reddish spot on the man's head. "He was hit over the head with a blunt object. Hit from behind, too. Likely fractured the skull and death would have been instantaneous."

Chase glanced around the messy living room: the tattered couch that had seen better days, the floral chintz curtains, the fast food cartons on the floor, the coffee table loaded with beer cans and the ashtrays filled to overflowing. It was clear that Mr. Dornhauser was a man who had believed in living dangerously, and hadn't been taking advantage of the Surgeon General's health advice. But what had ultimately killed him weren't the cigarettes he'd obviously been fond of, or the beer, but a vicious smack on the head.

"Any sign of the murder weapon?" asked Odelia as she walked in.

"Nothing," said Chase. Both he and Odelia had donned plastic gloves, and were deftly going through the man's stuff.

"Do you think we should wear plastic gloves, Max?" asked Dooley.

"I don't think so, Dooley."

"But what if we contaminate the evidence!"

"I don't think that's an issue," I said with a smile. You see, cats don't have fingers, so we don't have fingerprints either. We do have pawprints, but those are easily eliminated from the investigation.

"Weird," said Chase as he rifled through what looked like a small desk in the corner of the room.

"What is?" asked Odelia.

"No phone, no computer."

"Maybe he didn't have a phone or a computer?"

"He had an internet connection. And how many people do you know who don't have a phone nowadays?"

"None?"

"And what have we here?" the detective murmured as he stuck his hands into the man's jacket pocket and came away with a wallet.

"Can he do that, Max?" asked Dooley, referring to Chase looking through the man's wallet with keen interest.

"They're conducting a murder investigation," I pointed out. "So I think it's fine."

"But isn't this man entitled to privacy?"

"This man is dead, Dooley, and right now it's more important to catch his killer than to protect his privacy."

"Oh, right," said Dooley as he, too, glanced around, then sniffed the air. "It smells very bad in here, Max. I think they probably should open a window."

"Yeah, it does smell pretty terrible in here," I agreed. The smell of thousands of cigarettes having been smoked in this very room. And the stench of stale beer, of course.

"Look at this," said Chase, as he held out a neat stack of crisp twenty-dollar bills.

"Do you think…" Odelia began, as she took out her tablet and brought up a note she'd made. Odelia is a modern detective, you see. Used to be that police officers jotted everything down with pencil and paper, and Chase still does, but Odelia has one of those tablets on which you can write with a stylus. She and Chase now stood bent over her tablet, while they compared something on the screen to the bills Chase had liberated from Mr. Dornhauser's wallet. Then they both looked up, a smile on their faces.

"Bingo," said Chase.

"What's going on?" asked Dooley.

"It wouldn't surprise me," I said, "if the bills in Willie Dornhauser's wallet are the same ones Rosa Bond paid to her blackmailer last night." I now remembered that Odelia had instructed Rosa to have the bank write down the numbers on the notes they gave her.

"Absolutely right, Max," said Odelia, throwing caution to the wind and for once talking to us even when in the presence of others. She immediately regretted it, though, for Abe Cornwall had pricked up his ears and stood regarding us curiously. But then one of the techies drew his attention and they disappeared into the kitchen together.

"So Willie Dornhauser was Rosa Bond's blackmailer, huh?" said Chase.

"So where is the rest of the money?" asked Odelia.

Chase quickly counted the small stack he'd discovered in the dead man's wallet. "There's five hundred here. So that leaves four thousand five hundred unaccounted for."

And so they proceeded to turn the place upside down, looking for the rest of Rosa's money. When an hour had passed, and both the police and the crime scene technicians had searched everywhere, and the money still hadn't been found, Chase removed his plastic gloves and walked out to confer with his wife. We followed them out into the front yard, where a hushed conversation was carried out.

"Could be that he wasn't working alone," Chase suggested. "In which case his associate and Willie might have gotten into some kind of argument over how to split the money."

"The associate conked him on the head," said Odelia, describing a possible scenario, "and got away with the rest of the cash."

"Or could be that somehow Rosa discovered her blackmailer's identity, followed him here last night, and decided to exact some personal justice."

"Rosa isn't the vigilante type, Chase," said Odelia. "Besides, if she'd known who her blackmailer was, don't you think she would have told me?"

"We won't know until we talk to her," said Chase, very reasonably, I thought. He glanced up and down the street, where several people had gathered on the sidewalk, and stood talking animatedly, probably wondering what all the police activity was about. "First let's do a house-to-house, and find out who Willie Dornhauser was."

CHAPTER 9

Two of the people who had gathered in front of their house were Marge and Tex. So it stood to reason that we talked to them first. They'd lived on this street ever since they got married twenty-five years ago, and probably knew pretty much everybody on this block.

"Willie?" said Marge, looking surprised. "Yeah, of course I knew Willie. Great handyman."

"Yeah, he was," Tex confirmed. "Though we stopped using him a long time ago, didn't we, honey?"

"And why is that?" asked Chase.

"Well, Willie had a bad reputation," said Tex.

"What kind of reputation?"

"Let's just say that when you hired Willie to work on your house, things had a habit of disappearing."

"You mean he was a thief?"

"You can say that," said Tex, "though nothing was ever proven, and we never filed a complaint against him. We just stopped using him."

"The thing is that Willie had hands of gold," said Marge. "If you wanted something done in the house, and you asked

Willie, he got it done without any fuss, and he wasn't expensive either. Just…"

"That things got stolen," Chase completed the sentence.

Marge nodded. "It's a pity, because he was very talented."

"Willie did everything," said Tex. "Electricity, heating, plumbing… When you wanted a wall stuccoed, Willie could do it in a flash. When your air conditioner broke down, he fixed it. He installed new windows, put in a new floor, driveway…"

"The man could do absolutely everything," said Marge, nodding.

"So most people just put up with the occasional thing going missing," Tex said with a shrug.

"But not us," said Marge, "since the thing he stole when he worked at our house was very valuable to us." She glanced to her husband, a little smile played about her lips.

"He stole one of my gnomes," said Tex, and he wasn't smiling.

Tex is a big fan of gnomes, you see, and when you touch his gnomes, you touch a nerve with the good doctor.

"Did he also have a reputation as a blackmailer?" asked Chase.

Marge frowned. "Blackmail? No, I never heard that."

"Could be that lately he'd run out of customers," Tex suggested, "and that he had to resort to some more illegal activities to supplement his income."

"No matter how good you are at your job, at some point people get fed up," Marge pointed out, "and stop hiring you."

We moved to the house next door, where Kurt Mayfield lives, a retired music teacher. He seemed reluctant to talk to us, but when Chase reminded him that this was official police business, and not just a friendly neighborly chat across the fence, he stepped out onto the sidewalk. Up and down the street we could see other officers also conducting interviews with Willie Dornhauser's neighbors, and Kurt frowned when he noticed all the activity. "What's going on?" he asked. "Someone's house got burgled last night?"

"No, Kurt, a neighbor was found dead this morning," said Odelia.

"Dead!" The man's eyes had gone wide. "Who?"

"Willie Dornhauser," said Chase.

"Willie Dorn...," said Kurt thoughtfully. "Oh, right—the handyman."

"Did Willie ever do any work on your place, Kurt?" asked Chase.

"Nah, the man never set foot inside here. He had a bad rep, you see. For thieving."

"Yeah, we heard that," said Odelia. "Did you know him well?"

"Not really. I like to keep myself to myself, you know."

"Yeah, we do know," I murmured, causing Kurt to glance down and give me a sort of withering look. Kurt isn't into cats. Behind him, his Yorkshire Terrier had tripped up. Contrary to Kurt, Fifi is blessed with a sunny personality, and I'm always glad to see her.

"Hey, Max," she said. "Dooley. What's going on?"

"One of the neighbors got killed last night," I said.

"Oh, no!" she cried. "Was it a dog or a cat?"

"A human."

"Oh, no! Was it a man or a woman?"

"A man."

"Figures," she said.

"Figures how?"

"Well, it's always men who get in trouble with the law, isn't it? Must have something to do with the hormones."

"He didn't get in trouble with the law," I pointed out. "He

was murdered. Must have happened late last night. According to the coroner between midnight and three o'clock."

"I was sound asleep," she said, "and so was Kurt."

"Kurt isn't really a suspect," I said.

"He's not? Oh, phew. That's a load off my mind."

"Do you think Kurt is capable of murder?" asked Dooley.

"Oh, sure. He's got a short fuse, and when provoked can get upset. Not that he's ever mean to me," she was quick to add. "In fact I've never known a kinder man than Kurt."

"He's probably one of those humans who like dogs better than their fellow humans," Dooley said.

We all glanced up at Kurt and saw how gruff he was to Chase and Odelia, answering their questions with great reluctance.

"Yeah, he's not Mr. Sociable, is he?" I said.

"Not really," Fifi admitted. "I think he's never happier than when alone in the house with me, the television playing, and seated in his favorite chair with his—"

"With his microwave dinner on his lap?" I completed the sentence.

"Oh, no, Kurt doesn't do microwave dinners. He loves to cook. In fact he cooks every night. And he's a great cook, too. He often lets me sample the stuff he makes, and it's never anything short of absolute heaven."

Once more I glanced up at that gray-haired retired teacher. His glasses were perched on the tip of a bulbous nose, he was dressed in corduroy slacks and a beige waistcoat, and looked as gruff and unneighborly as ever. The image of the man didn't exactly jibe with the one Fifi was painting. Then again, what exactly did we know about the guy? Not much, except that he didn't like it when we rehearsed our cat choir repertoire in the backyard. He'd thrown the odd shoe or two in our direction in the past. But if he loved dogs, he couldn't be all bad, could he?

"If you want me to help you find the killer, just say the word, you guys," said Fifi. She sighed. "It gets boring just sitting at home and going out twice a day for a walk. I could do with a bit of excitement, to be perfectly honest."

"Sure," I said. "If you see or hear anything about Willie, anything at all, please tell us."

"Oh, absolutely," she said. "He didn't have a pet by any chance, did he?"

"No, unfortunately he didn't."

If he had, it would have made our jobs that much easier. A cat or dog belonging to Willie would have been able to tell us exactly what had transpired last night. Now all we could do was some good old-fashioned police work to find out what was going on.

"One thing we do know for sure," said Dooley, "is that Willie was a blackmailer."

"A blackmailer!" said Fifi, her eyes shining excitedly. "Oh, my."

"He was blackmailing Odelia's client." And we proceeded to give Fifi the short version of the events as they transpired the day before. She was duly impressed by the fascinating tale, and promised to let us know if she heard anything relating to Willie's murder.

CHAPTER 10

We moved to the house next to Marge and Tex, where Ted and Marcie Trapper already stood talking to an unknown female. When we walked up to the small group, the woman smiled at Chase and said, "Mr. and Mrs. Trapper knew Mr. Dornhauser well, detective." Chase stared at the woman, and no recognition registered on his face, so her smile faltered somewhat and a blush crept up her cheeks. "I'm sorry, sir. Sally Mortensen."

"Officer Mortensen, of course," said Chase, though clearly he had no idea who she was.

"I'll go and interview the people next door," she murmured, and hurried off.

"A new colleague?" asked Odelia.

"Looks like," said Chase. "I didn't recognize her." He turned to the Trappers. "I'm sorry, Ted—Marcie, but what can you tell us about Willie Dornhauser?"

"I think he did some work on the house not so long ago," said Ted. He turned to his wife with a quizzical look on his face. "Or am I thinking of some other person, honey?"

"No, I remember him well," said Marcie as she stared at

the picture Chase was holding up to her. "He fixed the roof. And after the job was finished, he broke into the house."

"I'm sorry, but are you saying Willie broke into your house?" asked Chase.

"We don't know it was him, Marcie," said Ted.

"The hell we don't. Who else could it be?"

"Did you go to the police?" asked Odelia.

"We did, yes," said Ted.

"Nothing ever came of it," said Marcie, who'd folded her arms across her chest and looked angry at the memory.

"What was stolen?"

"Not much," said Ted, who looked almost apologetic. "Just some money."

"And my rings!" said Marcie. "Don't forget about my rings!"

"Did you give a description when you filed a report?" asked Chase.

"I certainly did, and provided pictures, too."

Chase and Odelia shared a look. "We're checking Willie's house right now," said Chase.

"If you find my rings, I'd like to have them back."

"Like I said," Ted said, "we don't know it was Willie."

"Look, when you talk to the other people on this block you'll hear the same story over and over again," said Marcie. "Willie did some work on the house, then the next night, or at least within the week, the house would be burgled and stuff would be stolen. And okay, so maybe he was never caught, so we can't know for sure it was him, but I'm pretty sure it was. I mean, what are the odds?"

"Could be that he was staking out the place for a partner," Chase suggested.

"Could be," Marcie agreed. "But whoever it was, those burglaries had something to do with Willie. And you'll see that now that he's gone, those burglaries will magically stop."

"Unless his partner is still at it," said Odelia.

"Do you know if he was also into blackmail?" asked Chase.

Marcie shook her head decidedly. "I don't know anything about that. Though it wouldn't surprise me."

"I think Willie got involved with a bad crowd," said Ted. "I always found him an agreeable sort of person. And the man had hands of gold."

"That's true," said Marcie. "Willie could do anything. And the work was always great. Then again, I never had any complaints about his work. What I didn't like was him breaking in and stealing my rings."

"And my gnome," Ted said quietly.

Like Tex, Ted is a big gnome aficionado, and loves his gnomes almost more than he does his wife. Then again, aren't a lot of men like that? They dive headfirst into some weird hobby, and never look back. Ted and Tex have their gnomes, but other men collect cigar bands, or stamps, or toy trains. Or comics or soap bars or everything Coca Cola. Lucky for us Odelia had married a man who suffered from none of these quirks. Chase just liked to spend time with our human when he came home after a long day at the office. And of course he was proud of his arrest record. But there's nothing wrong with that.

"Who was the officer that Chase didn't know, Max?" asked Dooley as our humans thanked the Trappers for their cooperation and moved on to the next neighbor.

"I don't know, Dooley, and I guess Chase doesn't either."

"I think she's probably one of those invisible colleagues," my friend remarked.

"Invisible colleagues?"

"There are always colleagues that nobody notices, aren't there?" he said. "They work diligently at their desk for years, but they are, well, invisible."

"You don't mean that literally, do you?" I asked, just to make sure.

"No, of course not," he said with a laugh. "I just mean that nobody seems to take any notice of them. They do the work, but stay in the background. Like this officer. Probably she's been working at the precinct for months, or even years, but Chase has never seen her before—nobody has noticed her, and that's because she's one of the invisible ones."

He had a point, of course. There're always colleagues everybody notices, and then there are the ones who stay in the background, unobtrusively putting in the hours.

Just then, Uncle Alec came driving up, and called his deputy and Odelia over for a quick chat. "And?" said the Chief, crawling out of his car with some effort. His belly had gotten stuck behind the steering wheel, and he had trouble getting it unstuck. "Any luck?"

"Well, as far as we can tell Willie Dornhauser was a handyman with a particular hobby," said Chase, leaning against the hood of the car while Uncle Alec hoisted up his pants.

"Stealing from the people who hired him," Odelia clarified. "He would fix their heating and then a couple of days later he'd break into the place and steal their valuables."

"He was never arrested, though," said Chase, "which either makes him very good at what he did…."

"Or very lucky," said Odelia.

"Or he had an associate who did the dirty work," Chase said.

"I think you're right there, son," the Chief grunted. He handed a piece of paper to Chase. "I did some digging, and turns out that Willie was arrested once, ten years ago, for a B&E, and served time with this guy." He tapped the document.

"Edwardo Yuhas," Chase read.

"And Edwardo is not a stranger to the Hampton Cove PD," said Uncle Alec. "His MO was to break in and abscond with people's valuables. And a lot of his victims were located in this very neighborhood, until he moved on to other, more affluent parts of town."

"This could very well be Willie's partner," said Chase, nodding.

"Better go and have a chat with Mr. Yuhas," said Uncle Alec.

CHAPTER 11

As we passed back to the house, I saw how Harriet and Brutus were in congregation with Gran and Scarlett, no doubt discussing their new venture. Unfortunately I didn't have time to listen in, for Odelia and Chase were anxious to visit the address Uncle Alec had provided, and have a word with Willie's former—or current—criminal associate.

"What are Brutus and Harriet up to, Max?" asked Dooley as we were whisked away in Chase's squad car.

"The Baker Street Cats, Dooley," I said. "What else?"

"Why cats?" asked Dooley. "Why not Baker Street Pets?"

"I don't know, Dooley. Maybe they feel that only cats make good detectives?"

"I think any pet can be a good detective," said my friend. "Dogs are great at sniffing out clues, and birds have a great overview of what goes on beneath them, as they fly from tree to tree, or perch on rooftops, and imagine what a valuable source of information a gerbil could make? Or a hamster or even a goldfish? When they say that walls have ears, what people actually mean is that pets have ears—and pets are literally everywhere."

"You're absolutely right."

"I'll tell Brutus to include them in his new network."

"His army, you mean."

Odelia turned to us. "What's all this about Brutus's army?" she asked.

"Brutus wants to train an army of cats who'll be deployed to look for criminals," I explained.

"And Brutus will be the general of this army?"

"Something like that."

"So if Brutus is the general, what does that make Harriet?"

"Um… the general's wife?" Dooley suggested.

"No, Harriet will be in charge of training humans to talk to cats," I said.

Odelia's eyebrows shot up into her fringe. "Training humans to talk to cats!"

"Yeah, Gran believes that for the new neighborhood watch to succeed, all its members should be able to talk to cats, so cats can tell them all the little bits of gossip they spy out. All of this will be fed into one big database, and on top of this database an app will sit, constructed by Scarlett's computer-savvy grandnephew Kevin, and once everything is up and running, they'll sell it to Microsoft or Google for a hundred million dollars."

Odelia stared at me as if I'd lost my mind. "Max, are you serious?"

"Absolutely," I said. "A solid plan, no?" I added with a smile.

"A cockamamie plan," she remarked, turning back to face the front.

"What are they talking about?" asked Chase.

"Gran has hatched out another get-rich-quick scheme. This time it involves an app, an army of cats, and language lessons to learn to understand cats."

"But I thought your gift couldn't be taught?"

"Tell that to my grandmother. Apparently she thinks differently."

We'd arrived at the house of Willie's former cellmate, and got out. The house was in a not-so-nice part of town, where all the houses looked like the one where Willie lived. Only this particular house looked even more rundown than the others. And when Chase rang the bell, there was no reply.

"His name is on the bell," the cop grunted as he glanced through the window in an attempt to locate the tenant.

And since a good cop is never beaten, he rang the bell of Edwardo Yuhas's next-door neighbor. An old man came shuffling to the fore, and gave Chase a kindly smile.

"Edwardo? Oh, he doesn't live here anymore, detective."

"When did he move out?"

"He didn't move out. He was kicked out, for being late with the rent."

"And when was this?"

"Oh, let me think. Must be six months now, maybe more." He jerked his thumb to the house next door. "House needs work, don't you think? Can't you go and talk to the owner? Ask him to tear the whole place down and just build a new one?"

Chase smiled at the pensioner. "I'm afraid I can't do that, sir."

"Well, you should. It's a damn shame the way they let this whole neighborhood go to the dogs. Soon the houses will start falling down all by themselves."

And shaking his head he shuffled inside again, closing the door behind him.

Chase scratched his scalp. "Maybe we can talk to the owner?" he said. "Ask him if Edwardo left a forwarding address?"

We glanced around, and I said, "I think I can do you one

better, Chase," and approached a stray cat licking its behind nearby. "Hey there, buddy," I said.

The cat looked up and gave me a suspicious look. "What do you want?" he asked.

"Cool your jets," I said. "I just want some information about a guy who used to live here."

"And why would I tell you anything?"

"Because you're a cat, and I'm a cat, and us cats should stick together and help each other out, wouldn't you agree?"

"No, I wouldn't," he said. I noticed how his tail looked a little ratty, and his ear looked as if someone had taken a big bite out of it at some point.

"Look, a man has been killed," I said, "and we are trying to find out what happened."

He shrugged, indicating he didn't really care one way or another.

"Are you part of the Baker Street Cats?" asked Dooley, also wandering up.

"Baker Street what?" asked the cat with a frown.

"Brutus's army," Dooley clarified.

"I don't know any Brutus, and I don't know any army, so just get lost already, will you?"

"Do you know Clarice, by any chance?" I asked, deciding to try a different tack.

This time a gleam of interest appeared in his pale green eyes. "Sure I know Clarice. She's a legend around these parts. Why, do you know her?"

"She's a great friend of ours," I said.

"Why didn't you say so!" he cried, and suddenly his whole demeanor changed. "Any friend of Clarice is a friend of mine. It's been a long time since she showed her face around here."

"I have to admit I haven't seen her in a while either," I said.

"She used to hang out a lot in Dumpster City," he said.

"Dumpster City?"

"Main Street is what the locals call it. Plenty of dumpsters out there. So what do you wanna know?"

"The guy who used to live here," I said, pointing to Edwardo's last-known address. "Any idea where we might find him?"

"Best bet would be the Generals Arms," he said.

"Is that a bar?"

"Yeah, not a very nice one, mind you. But it's where he spends most of his time. Him and some of his seedy friends."

"Thanks…"

"Barry Gibb," said the cat.

"Barry Gibb?"

"Yeah. On account of my great singing voice." He suddenly puffed himself up and started belting out, *"Well, you can tell by the way I use my walk I'm a woman's man."*

"Thanks, Barry Gibb," I said quickly.

"Hey, it's all about stayin' alive, buddy."

"Absolutely."

"Tell Clarice I said hi, will you?"

"I will," I said as we returned to Chase and Odelia, who stood patiently waiting.

"And tell her not to be a stranger!" Barry Gibb cried after us, and I lifted my paw in response.

"Nice fellow, Barry Gibb," said Dooley.

"Yeah, very nice," I agreed.

"Let's ask him to join cat choir."

"Let's not." And addressing my human, I said, "Generals Arms. It's a bar where Edwardo hangs out a lot."

Odelia's smile was something to behold. "Thanks, Max. I owe you one."

CHAPTER 12

We waited outside while Chase and Odelia walked into the Generals Arms to talk to the bartender. Strange as it may sound, but some of these bars and restaurants have a No Pets Allowed policy. It's not something I'll ever be able to understand, though of course it is true that pets usually don't carry wallets and so don't make the best customers. And since these places only make money when the patrons pay for their services, I guess there is a certain logic to barring pets from frequenting them.

"Do you think that the Baker Street Cats will make police work a thing of the past, Max?" asked Dooley as we waited on the sidewalk like the good assistants that we were.

"I don't think so, Dooley," I said.

"But why, Max? If all the cats in all the cities in all the world are mobilized to hunt criminals, there will be no more crime, and the police will find themselves out of a job."

"There's a lot of stuff the police do that has nothing to do with crime, Dooley," I said.

"Like what?"

"Directing traffic, for instance," I said after a moment's

reflection. "Or crowd control."

"I don't think Chase will be happy to go from being a detective to directing traffic."

"No, well, I don't think it will ever come to that."

Odelia and Chase had come walking out of the bar, both looking relieved.

"We got him," said Odelia. "Turns out he was in here with Willie last night, huddling in a corner for a long time, before apparently getting into some kind of fight. They had to break them up, and they were hurling a string of expletives in each other's direction."

"But why?" I asked.

Odelia shrugged. "The bartender said that Edwardo accused Willie of betraying him, though what exactly the argument was about, he didn't know. All he knows is that he kicked both men out, and that's the last time he saw them."

"Let's go," said Chase curtly, as he tucked his notebook back into his jacket pocket.

Moments later we were zooming along in the direction of Edwardo's new place, and when we arrived there, discovered it was actually a deserted old factory.

"The people who claim that crime doesn't pay would get a kick out of this," Chase grunted when he took in the rundown old building, where, according to the markings on the facade, once wheelbarrows had been made.

"Looks like Willie's friend has hit hard times," Odelia remarked.

We all got out and approached the industrial structure. Entering the place, we found the entrance strewn with plenty of rubble, and as we proceeded deeper into the heart of the factory, it soon became clear that several people had selected it as their home. Mattresses had been placed on the concrete floor, and someone had even started a fire. The fire was out now, fortunately, but if this went on they might as

PURRFECT LIFE

well set fire to the whole building… which frankly speaking might not be such a bad idea, as an old eyesore like this could only have one purpose: to be torn down to make room for new housing.

As Odelia went in one direction and Chase in another, Dooley and I decided to simply wander around, and let our intuition be our guide. Our intuition has served us well in the past, you see, and I hoped it would serve us well this time. And soon I picked up the scent of food being broiled or boiled, and so naturally we proceeded in that direction.

"I think I'm hungry, Max," said my friend.

"You think you're hungry or you are hungry?" I asked as I studied our surroundings. The factory might have been deserted, but some of the old machinery had been left in place. I even saw several wheelbarrows piled up in a corner. Odd that a wheelbarrow factory would go bust, I thought. Who doesn't like a nice shiny wheelbarrow?

And then we spotted him: a man cooking something on a portable gas stove. When he saw us, he frowned. "Shoo," he said, and picked up a rock and threw it in our direction!

"Do you think this is Edwardo, Max?" I asked Dooley.

"I don't know, Dooley," I said, "but if it is, and he did steal four thousand five hundred dollars from his friend, he's not spending it on a gourmet meal."

Suddenly, Chase appeared on the other side of the cavernous space and called out, "Police. Have you seen Edwardo Yuhas, sir?"

The man cursed under his breath, and immediately got up and started running in our direction.

Now I know that when a large man runs in your direction the first instinct is to flee, and I must confess I experienced a momentary temptation to do just that, but then I steeled myself to the task, and instead of running away from the danger, actually ran toward it! Though I think the rock-throwing might have had something to do with this as well. And so as my path crossed with that of the man, he sort of tripped over me and fell to the concrete floor. Moments later, Chase was upon him, and held him down.

"Hey, you can't do that!" the man cried. "This is police brutality!"

"Relax, buddy," said Chase. "I just want to know where I can find Edwardo Yuhas, that's all—hold on, you're Edwardo Yuhas, aren't you?" he said, checking the man's credentials.

"And what if I am?" said the man, who had a large head, and an even larger body.

Odelia, attracted by the noise, now also come running up, and helped Chase to go through the man's pockets. When she extracted a nice wad of cash from his coat pocket, all crisp new bills, she smiled.

"Now where does a man with no fixed abode come into such a nice sum of money, Mr. Yuhas?" asked Chase, still holding the man down.

"I'm not telling you a thing, cop," said Mr. Yuhas.

"Did you hurt yourself, Max?" asked Dooley solicitously.

"No, I'm fine," I said. I'd survived a run-in with Brutus last night, so running into Mr. Yuhas was starting to feel like my regular shtick.

"Here's more," said Odelia, who'd opened the man's backpack and now showed us a plastic bag with more money inside.

"Hey, that's Rosa's plastic bag," I said.

Odelia showed Edwardo the plastic bag with the money. "I think you have some explaining to do, buddy," she said.

"I found that," said Edwardo. "I found it on the street. So finders keepers, you know."

"Of course you did," said Chase, and hauled the man to his feet, then supplied him with a nice pair of handcuffs, and read him his rights.

CHAPTER 13

The ride to the precinct was an awkward one, for Dooley and I had to share the backseat with this cuffed criminal. Especially the fact that he kept throwing very nasty glances in my direction unnerved me a great deal. I guess he was still upset that I'd tripped him up, and presumably blamed me for his capture.

Once arrived, I felt relieved when Chase removed the man from the car, and escorted him into the police station, to interrogate him in the proper circumstances, and get his statement down on paper. Signed, sealed and delivered—another crime solved.

Unfortunately, and in spite of my natural curiosity, cats aren't allowed into the interview rooms, and so we were dependent on Odelia to supply us with the information as to the conclusion of the interview. And since Odelia isn't an actual cop, she wasn't allowed to sit in on the interview either. She was, however, allowed to follow along from the next room, where a one-way mirror offers a very nice view of the interrogation.

Forced to wait in Chase's office, Dooley and I made

ourselves comfortable on Chase's small but cozy sofa, and soon curled up into two respective balls and succumbed to a refreshing nap. When Chase and Odelia entered the office, immediately I was wide awake.

"He confessed," Odelia announced. "But only for taking the money, not the murder."

"I think if I keep leaning on him he'll confess to the murder as well," Chase said as he took a seat behind his desk and opened his laptop, presumably to start typing up a report.

It's not enough that cops catch the criminals, you see, they also have to write all kinds of reports when they do, and sometimes the paperwork associated with an arrest takes them more time than to actually make the arrest in the first place.

"So he admitted that he was in on the blackmail?" I asked.

"Not the blackmail," said Odelia as she took a seat in front of her husband's desk and addressed us. "He didn't know about the blackmail. He did confess that he and Willie had a nice business going for a while: Willie would be hired as a handyman, stake out the place, and Edwardo would break in and take the stuff Willie had selected. But lately they'd fallen out, over some money that Edwardo said Willie owed him. So when Willie didn't answer his phone, he paid him a visit and found his former partner dead on the floor."

"He didn't kill him?"

"That's what he says. He says he found him dead, then decided to search the place, like any good friend would. And that's when he found the plastic bag with the blackmail money and took it."

"I don't believe a word the guy says," said Chase. "I think the part about them falling out is true. And so when Edwardo dropped by last night, they got into yet another fight, only this time he hit his ex-partner over the head, grabbed the money and ran."

"So where is Willie's phone?"

Chase shrugged.

"He didn't have it?" I asked.

"Edwardo claims he didn't find Willie's phone," said Odelia.

"He probably took it and dumped it," said Chase, "to hide his connection with the guy."

"So where does that leave us?" I asked.

"That leaves us with a job well done," said Odelia, smiling and giving me a pat on the head. "Hats off to you, Max, for helping us catch the guy."

"So you think he did it?" asked Dooley. "He's the killer?"

"Yeah, I think that's pretty much a foregone conclusion. A falling-out amongst thieves, and one thief deciding to kill the other one and take the money."

"Rosa will be happy," I said.

"Yeah, not only does she get her money back," said Odelia, leaning back and rubbing her eyes, "but her blackmailer has effectively been put out of business."

"Unless Edwardo decides to take over from his partner," I said.

"I doubt it. Frankly I think he wasn't lying about that part. He really didn't seem to have a clue about the blackmail stuff Willie was into."

"No, he seemed completely oblivious," Chase confirmed. "And now if you'll excuse me," he said, cracking his knuckles, "I have a report to write."

"What do you think happened to Willie's phone?" I asked as we walked out.

"Like Chase said, Edwardo probably took it and dumped it."

"So case closed?" asked Dooley.

Odelia smiled. "Yes, honey. Case closed. And an extra treat for you guys tonight."

"Yay," said Dooley.

We returned to Odelia's office, where she, too, had some writing to do. While Chase slaved away over his report, she promptly settled in and started writing up an article about the murder of a handyman, and the arrest of his criminal associate. Meanwhile, Dooley and I settled down in the cozy little nook in her office she's reserved for us, and would have continued enjoying our much-deserved naptime, if not suddenly Odelia's phone had rung and the moment she saw who it was, put it on speaker.

"Odelia," said a voice that sounded familiar. "It's Rosa Bond. The most terrible thing has happened. My son has gone missing!"

CHAPTER 14

When we arrived at the house where the Bond family lives, I was pleasantly surprised to find it to be a nice big house in an affluent part of town. After the squalor we'd been confronted with all morning, it made for a nice change of pace.

The house wasn't just big, it also sported two garage ports, and the big Tesla parked in front of one indicated these people didn't stint for money.

The front door opened, and an anxious-looking Rosa greeted us and ushered us in.

"I don't know where he is," she said, not bothering with preliminaries. "I called the school about the upcoming summer bash, and they asked how Todd was doing. Turns out he called in sick yesterday."

"Sick?" asked Odelia as we were led into a spacious living room. The humans took their seats on the beige leather couches while Dooley and I found the fluffy carpet very agreeable.

"He didn't go to school this morning either," said Rosa. She had dark circles under her eyes, and it was clear this whole blackmail business had taken its toll. Coming upon that dreadful episode, her son's disappearance had hit her hard. "He handed in a doctor's note yesterday. Must have been a fake. Todd is very handy with the computer."

"So he didn't go to school yesterday or today?" asked Odelia.

Rosa nodded nervously. "And when he came home last night he was distracted and irritated. He snapped at me, and at his sister, and when I told him to apologize, he ignored me and went straight up to his room."

"Did he leave here this morning?"

"He did. He left at the usual time."

"And you have no idea where he could be."

Rosa hesitated, then said, "I think it must have something to do with his dad."

"You mean your husband?"

"No, his real dad. Lately he's been asking me a lot of questions about Clive. I've tried to ignore them, since I don't think it's fair to Tilton, but Todd insisted. Started rehashing that whole dreadful business."

"So what are you saying? That he's gone looking for his real dad?"

Rosa bit her lip and nodded. "That's what I'm afraid of. He talked about this years ago, when he was old enough to understand what happened, about finding his dad and asking him why he did what he did. But then the last couple of years he seemed to have accepted that his dad left us and I thought he'd dropped it. Only now it all started again."

"Remind me again how old Todd is?"

"Sixteen." She threw up her hands. "It could be his age. Boys his age need a father figure, maybe? I don't know, Odelia. I'm grasping at straws here."

"Did you try his phone?"

"Of course. He's not picking up."

"Maybe he's staying with a friend?"

"I've called all of the people I know, but they haven't seen him either."

"Did Todd talk to your husband? Maybe he told him what his plans are?"

"Oh, no. Todd and my husband are barely on speaking terms these days. Even though he respects Tilton, he has never accepted him as his dad."

"And how about his sister?"

Rosa automatically glanced up at the ceiling. "Todd and Aisha are very close. If he's confided in anyone, it would be her. But I've already asked her, and she says he didn't tell her what he was up to."

"Maybe I can talk to her?" Odelia suggested.

"Will you?" said Rosa, an anxious look in her eyes. "It's possible that she'll tell you more than she would me. She's fifteen, and she seems to have entered her rebellious phase. So now all of a sudden I'm the enemy."

"I'll give it a shot," said Odelia, and gave the woman a reassuring smile. "I'm sure Todd is fine. And I also think it's normal for a boy his age to wonder about his dad, and to want to go and look for him."

"But if he went down to Mexico…" said Rosa, and let her voice trail away. But the look of terror in her eyes spoke volumes. A boy of sixteen, alone in Mexico, looking for his dad, might run into all kinds of trouble.

"I'll talk to Aisha first, shall I? Maybe she knows something she's not telling you."

Rosa nodded, and got up. "Aisha!" she called out along the staircase. "Can you come down a minute, honey?"

"I'm busy, Mom!" the girl yelled back.

"It's important!" Rosa said, raising her voice, and giving Odelia an apologetic little smile. Teenagers, that smile seemed to say.

"Oh, fine!" the girl's voice came, full of exasperation,

and then we heard footsteps stomping down the stairs, and moments later a teenage girl appeared. She looked younger than her age, and was dressed in stylishly ripped jeans and a T-shirt announcing that she thought Bruno Mars was way cool, and giving Odelia a curious look. Then she saw Dooley and me, and she actually smiled. "Oh, nice!" she said, and immediately crouched down to give us both cuddles. In response, we started purring up a storm.

Obviously this was not a girl who was worried about her brother, so I felt that Odelia's mission might prove successful.

"This is Odelia Kingsley, sweetie," said Rosa. "I've asked her to look for Todd."

"Oh, Mom, I told you, Todd is probably staying with a friend, and he can't be bothered to answer your calls."

"What friend would that be?" asked Odelia.

The girl hesitated, and her fervor to caress Dooley and me quickly lessened and a cautious look came over her face. "I don't know. Todd has many friends."

"So you don't think he's run off to go look for his dad in Mexico?" asked Odelia.

"Oh, please. Of course not. He doesn't even speak Spanish."

"Your mom seems to feel that Todd has been talking a lot about his dad lately."

"So? That doesn't mean he's crazy enough to go look for him."

"So he didn't tell you where he was planning to go?"

Aisha shook her head. "He never tells me anything. He just goes off and does whatever he likes. Doesn't talk to me, or anyone."

"But you're his sister."

"So?" scoffed Aisha. "It's not as if he tells me his secrets."

"Secrets?" asked Rosa, panic clear in her voice. "Todd has secrets?"

"God, Mom, we all have secrets. It's no big deal."

"But what secrets?"

"How should I know? I just told you he never tells me anything."

"I understand he didn't go to school yesterday or today?" asked Odelia.

"So?" said Aisha evasively, clearly not eager to talk about her big brother's surprise departure.

"So why did he play hooky?"

Aisha shrugged.

"Has he done this before?"

Another shrug.

"Aisha, if you know something, you have got to tell us!" said Rosa.

"Look, I don't know anything, all right? And even if I did, he wouldn't want me to tell you. Now can you please get off my back!" And with these words, she stomped back up the stairs. Moments later, loud music made the ceiling vibrate. I think it may have been Bruno Mars, though since I'm not well-versed with the music choices of the current generation I wasn't entirely sure.

Rosa gave Odelia a look of apology. "I'm sorry," she said. "It's been a lot of this lately."

"Does Aisha get along with your husband?" asked Odelia.

"More or less. She accepts him, and respects him, but Aisha and her brother have told me from the beginning that they'll never call him Dad, or see him as their dad."

"And how does Tilton feel about that?"

"He's fine with it. He knows they'll never see him as their dad, and that's okay for him."

Suddenly a loud wailing sound came from a nanny cam located on the living room table, and Rosa said, "Looks like all this shouting has woken up the baby." And with a murmured apology, she disappeared upstairs, then moments later came down again, holding said baby, and gently rocking her in her arms.

"And who is this?" asked Odelia with a smile.

"Alisa," said Rosa, tenderness clear in both her voice and her expression.

"How old is she?"

"Eighteen months. The doctor told me I couldn't have another baby, and we'd already accepted that, until suddenly I discovered I was pregnant again. We call her our miracle baby." She addressed the infant. "You didn't care what the doctors said, did you? No, you decided to prove them all wrong." She turned to Odelia. "Do you have kids?"

"No, not yet," said Odelia. "We just got married a couple of months ago."

"Plans to have a family?"

Odelia nodded. "Yeah, absolutely."

Dooley and I shared a look of alarm.

"Max!" Dooley whispered. "Oh, no!"

CHAPTER 15

"There's one other thing we need to talk about, Rosa," said Odelia.

Rosa looked up at this, a questioning look in her eyes.

"The blackmail," said Odelia.

"You mean... there's news?"

Odelia smiled. "We caught him."

"You did?!"

"Yes. And we also recuperated the money. Unfortunately I won't be able to return it to you just yet, since it's now part of the investigation, and evidence in a murder inquiry."

"A murder inquiry!"

"Unfortunately, the man who was blackmailing you was found dead this morning. Apparently he'd gotten into a fight with his partner, and as far as we can ascertain the partner killed him and took the money. The man has been arrested, and we found the money in his possession."

"Oh, my God—who was he?"

"Well, the man who was blackmailing you was a local handyman named Willie Dornhauser, and his partner Edwardo Yuhas. Do any of these names ring a bell?"

Rosa thought for a moment, then shook her head, even as she was gently rocking her baby in her arms.

Odelia had taken out her phone, and now showed pictures of both men to Rosa.

"Oh, wait. I think I've seen this man before." She was pointing to the picture of Willie. "I think he did some work on our bathroom last summer. Is he…"

"Yes, he's the man who contacted you and arranged the pickup last night."

"But how did he know about…"

"Your ex-husband? I'm afraid we don't know yet. But his partner is being interrogated by my husband as we speak, and I'm sure he'll be able to tell us." She frowned. "Is it possible that when Mr. Dornhauser worked on your bathroom he happened to find some documents relating to your ex-husband, Rosa?"

"I don't think so. I got rid of all that years ago, when Clive ran off with his secretary. For a while I waited for him to get in touch, but months passed and finally I decided I needed to move on. When I did, I got rid of everything that reminded me of my old life."

"Maybe he overheard you and Tilton discussing your past?"

But Rosa shook her head adamantly. "Impossible."

"But I thought you said Tilton knows about your past?"

"He does, but when we got married I made him promise never to bring it up again. You see, before the wedding, I had a long conversation with Tilton, and told him who I was, and all that had happened with Clive and the money. I didn't want to move forward and build a marriage based on lies and deceit. But I also told him that we were going to have this conversation once and then we were going to let it rest."

"And he was okay with that?"

"Yes, and I'm still grateful to him to this day. He told me that I wasn't to blame for the things my ex-husband had done. And so we never discussed Clive or that dreadful business again." She gave Odelia a weak smile. "It's very rare to get a second chance, and I still thank my lucky stars that I was offered the opportunity to start over—and this time do it right."

"It wasn't your fault that your husband turned out to be a liar and a thief, Rosa."

"I know, but you can't help wonder, you know—wonder if somehow you're to blame for what happened. But Tilton was so wonderful about it. He said that our relationship was a way for me start over, and frankly I never looked back—until that phone call."

"Well, that's all over now," said Odelia, taking Rosa's hand and pressing it gently. "The man is dead, and his partner arrested. And as soon as the investigation is concluded, you will get that money back."

"It's not so much the money I'm worried about than the scandal that might follow if people in this town found out about Clive. And I'm not even concerned about myself," said Rosa, tenderly stroking a lock of angel hair on her baby's head. "I really don't care what happens to me. It's my children's future that would be jeopardized. And Todd and Aisha already went through so much. Even though they were young, they remember, you know."

"They still remember their dad?"

"Oh, yes, they do. You'd be surprised how much kids pick up, even when they're as young as Todd and Aisha were at the time." She gave Odelia a grateful look. "I can't thank you enough, Odelia."

"That's all right. I'm glad it all turned out well."

"Now if only Todd would come home," said Rosa, and

that pained look was back. "I just hope he doesn't do anything stupid."

"You're afraid he takes after his dad, aren't you?"

Rosa nodded, and her eyes grew moist. "Yes, I am. I'm afraid he might do something really foolish—just like Clive."

CHAPTER 16

We were on our way back into town, and frankly Dooley and I were too upset for speech. Odelia was going to have a baby! Now of all the shocking things that could have been laid at our paws, this was probably the most life-changing one to date—even more life-changing than the insertion into our lives of Chase, and with him, Brutus.

But since we didn't want to give vent to our shock and dismay in front of Odelia, we wisely kept our tongue, though the looks we gave each other spoke volumes. Good thing Odelia had to keep her eyes on the road, and didn't catch the wordless communication that was carried out between us.

"So what do you think, you guys?" she asked finally, once she'd had time to put all her ducks in a row after the long talk she had with Rosa. "Did Todd go off to Mexico to look for his dad, you think?"

"I doubt it," I said. "He's only sixteen, Odelia. Where would he get the money?"

"Yeah, and how would he hope to find his dad?" Odelia added. "It is a big country. Unless he already knew where he was going, of course," she added.

"You mean he might have been planning this for a while?"

"It is possible. It's been nine years, so maybe he's been digging into the mystery of his dad's disappearance for years now, and finally thinks he knows where to find him."

"Or maybe his dad got in touch with him," Dooley suggested. "And invited him over for a holiday."

"Oh, Dooley," said Odelia. "Now why would Clive sneak behind his ex-wife's back and invite his son over to his hideout?"

"Because he's a wanted man? And he doesn't want the police to find him?"

"He is a fugitive from justice," I agreed.

"Even so. Why invite his son, and not his daughter?" asked Odelia.

"Maybe he did invite Aisha," said Dooley. "She was acting really strange, wasn't she?"

"She was," I said. "So maybe she knows more than she's letting on."

"I did get the impression she was hiding something," Odelia agreed. "So maybe she does know where her brother is, but is refusing to tell her mom, or us."

"I still think that if the kid took off for Mexico, he would have left a trace," I said. "He'd need a passport, wouldn't he? And he'd need money. He'd also need a car. Or if he took a flight, there would be checks done at the airport. I really don't think a sixteen-year-old kid can just up and leave and cross the border without his parents being notified."

"Yeah, you're right," said Odelia. "If he did go off to Mexico in search of his dad, sooner or later we're bound to find out about it."

"I just hope he won't get shot ," said Dooley.

I gave him a look of concern, and so did Odelia through the rearview mirror.

"Well, Mexico is a dangerous country," Dooley argued. "People get shot or buried in unmarked graves all the time."

And with rising concern over young Todd's fate, Odelia parked her car across the street from a modern office building, and as she glanced over, she said, "Let's hope Todd's stepdad will be able to tell us more." She consulted her notes. "Tilton Bond. Started an internet business in 2011, sold it in 2016."

"What internet business was he in?" I asked.

"A financial and investing advice site, apparently. And a very successful one."

"Don't tell Gran," I said, "Or she'll want to start one of those herself."

"I doubt if there's still a lot of money to be made there. The market must be saturated with investment advice sites. Well, let's go and have a word with the former whizz kid."

The whizz kid didn't look like much of a whizz kid, I thought. Then again, his whizz kid days were a thing of the past now. Tilton Bond was a tall man, with a full crop of dark hair, graying at the temples, which lent him a distinguished look. He had a neatly trimmed beard, pale blue eyes that didn't miss a trick, and a charming demeanor overall.

"Please take a seat," he said, as he gestured to a chair in front of a large mahogany desk. He then glanced down at Dooley and myself, and Odelia was forced to explain our presence. She did it with the practiced ease of one who's had to explain the presence of her cats to many people many times. "Well, what can I do for you?" asked the man, giving her a pleasant smile.

"I just had a long talk with your wife," said Odelia. "And she told me that your stepson Todd has gone missing."

"Yes, well," said Tilton, his face taking on an appropriate look of concern. "It's not the first time he's done that, and it probably won't be the last. Todd is at an age where rebellion seems to be the best answer to just about everything that troubles him."

"Your wife seems to think he may have gone to Mexico, to look for his father."

Tilton quirked an eyebrow. "She told you about that, did she?"

"Yes, she came to me because of the blackmail."

"A dreadful business. You caught the scoundrel?"

"Yes, we did. Unfortunately when we found him he was already dead—killed by his associate."

"I know. I just got off the phone with your uncle, Mrs. Kingsley. He told me about the late Mr. Dornhauser and the things he was involved in."

"Do you think there's any connection between the blackmail and Todd's disappearance?"

"I doubt it. Like I said, it's not the first time Todd has gone missing. The last time was over a bad report card. His mother and I gave him some grief over that, and he couldn't think of a better way to respond than to disappear for an entire weekend. He'd convinced a friend of his that I was bullying him, and that he needed to hide."

"And did you? Bully him?"

"Of course not. I've only ever treated my wife's kids with the utmost respect. I love them as if they were my own—though it hasn't been easy. You see, when I met their mother, they'd just gone through a very traumatizing experience—with their dad deciding to become a bank robber, and gallivanting off to Mexico with his secretary and five million dollars of his clients' money. So the last thing they needed was for their mom to come home one day and announce she met a man, and was planning to marry him and move in together."

"Todd wasn't happy about that, was he?"

"Not at first, but I like to think he and I have grown closer over time. But sixteen is a difficult age for any boy, Mrs. Kingsley, and certainly for a young man who went through what Todd had to go through on account of his dad. But on the whole I think we all get along fine."

"What about Aisha?"

"What about her?"

"When Rosa asked her if she knew what her brother was up to, I had the impression she knew more than she was letting on."

"Oh, I wouldn't be surprised if she does. You see, Todd and Aisha have always been very close. Again because of the trauma they shared. The last time Todd went off without telling us where he was, Aisha was the only person he'd confided in."

"So you think he's staying with a friend again this time?"

"Yes, I do."

"So the story about Mexico…"

Tilton gave us an indulgent smile. "I hardly think a boy his age would have the means or the initiative to launch an international search for his missing father, Mrs. Kingsley."

"It's possible his dad got in touch, and gave him his address," Odelia suggested.

"Yes, I guess it is possible," said Mr. Bond. "But then I'd ask myself why he'd wait nine years to get in touch. Why now, all of a sudden? And why not simply talk to Rosa?"

"Because he's afraid she'll turn him in to the police?"

"Well, she would, of course," Tilton agreed. "Considering the grief that man put her and the kids through." He thought for a moment, then decidedly shook his head. "No, I'm sure Todd is staying with a friend again, and he'll be home in one or two days, blaming us for whatever it is that upset him this time." He smiled. "Do you have kids, Mrs. Kingsley?"

"That question again!" Dooley hissed. "Why do they keep wanting her to have kids!"

"Because that's what most people who get married do, Dooley," I whispered back. "They get married and have kids!"

"Well, not Odelia—she already has us!"

"No, not at the moment," said Odelia with a smile.

"Wait till they suddenly turn from delightful little angels into monstrous teenagers. Friends tell me that it will all pass soon enough, and we shouldn't worry too much. Though I don't mind telling you I hope it will pass sooner rather than later."

"If you don't mind me asking, sir," said Odelia, "but did you ever have second thoughts about marrying Rosa—knowing about her history?"

Tilton's smile widened. "Never. Not for one second. You see, the moment I laid eyes on her, I knew she was the one for me—even if she didn't know it herself. I was forty at the time, long past the age when people fall in love at first sight. In fact I always thought that was just a lot of nonsense. I spent my life building a successful business, and never had time for romance. Until I met Rosa, and I could have sworn my heart stopped for a moment, then fortunately started up again."

"And what about taking on two kids of another man—a man guilty of a crime?"

"Rosa is blameless in all of this. She didn't know what her husband was up to. Before the wedding she said she had something very important to tell me, and she was going to tell me now, so I could still back out of the wedding if I wanted to." He glanced to a framed picture on his desk, a family portrait of himself, Rosa, Todd and Aisha. "I didn't even have to think twice. I told her then what I still feel strongly now: she was never to blame for what her husband did. On the contrary, she was as much a victim of her husband's crime as the people he stole from."

"That was very noble of you, sir."

"Not at all. I was in love, you see, but not so bedazzled that I didn't have a private detective look into Rosa's past. A man in my position has to be careful. But he told me what I already knew in my heart: she never had an inkling of what Clive was up to. And after he disappeared, he didn't even try to get in touch. Abandoned his family without a second thought." His expression hardened. "Which makes me despise him even more."

The interview was over, and we all got up. Odelia shook Mr. Bond's hand. "What do you do these days, sir? As I understand, you don't have to work for a living anymore."

He laughed. "You mean, why do I have an office if I'm independently wealthy?"

"Something like that."

"Well, a wealthy man suddenly becomes very popular, Mrs. Kingsley, and any number of charities and organizations suddenly pop out of the woodwork, eager to share your wealth with you. And so after I made a careful selection, I decided to award a few of them with my patronage and my money. So now I find myself on so many committees that I have to work harder than when I was still building my business. But you know what?" He leaned in as he shook Odelia's hand warmly. "It's so much more enjoyable now that I get to pick and choose what to do with my time—and my money, of course."

As we left the office, and found ourselves on the sidewalk once more, Odelia said, "He wasn't lying. According to an article I read, Tilton Bond is one of the most generous contributors to Hampton Cove's many charities and nonprofits, and practically singlehandedly keeps them all running."

"The world needs more people like him," I said.

"It sure does," she agreed.

CHAPTER 17

That evening, we were scheduled to go out patrolling with the neighborhood watch. Though I should probably call it the Baker Street Cats, since that was the new name.

Before setting out to patrol the streets and alleys that form our small town, Scarlett and Gran sat down with the four of us in Tex and Marge's backyard, for another installment in what apparently were a series of lessons to teach Scarlett our language.

"My name is Harriet," said Harriet emphatically, enunciating every syllable clearly.

"Meow meow meow," said Scarlett, managing to look bewildered, frustrated and puzzled at the same time.

"No, no, no," said Harriet.

"Meow meow meow," Scarlett said once more.

"You're not listening," said Harriet. "Repeat after me: My name is Harriet."

"Meow meow meow etcetera," said Scarlett. She looked to Gran, who sat consulting her smartphone. "Do you have any idea what she's saying?"

"She said 'My name is Harriet,'" Gran murmured. "And

then she said you're not listening, and she repeated: 'My name is Harriet.'"

"Well, all I'm hearing is a lot of meowing, and it all sounds the same."

"It's not, darling. She's forming very distinct words, and those words all form distinct and clearly defined sentences, and when you put it all together, there is a very clear and distinct meaning in those words and sentences."

"But it all sounds like gibberish to me! And will you please put down that damned phone!"

"There seems to be a lot of criminal activity going on in our town," Gran said. "A television set was stolen from Mrs. Barker on Lincoln Street. And two vandals were caught in the act of spraying graffiti on a car belonging to a Mr. Monsoon." She sighed. "We really need to get out there and start patrolling, or else this whole place will go down in flames."

"You're not listening to a word I'm saying, Vesta. I can't do this—it's impossible!"

"No, it's not. You're simply not trying hard enough. Now repeat after me. My name is Harriet."

"Meow meow meow," said Scarlett, rolling her eyes.

"No, that's not it. I clearly said 'My name is Harriet.'"

"That's not what I heard."

"Then you heard wrong." Gran glanced to her friend's ears. "Maybe it's your hearing. Are you sure you don't need a hearing aid?"

"There's nothing wrong with my ears, Vesta."

"You're not as young as you used to be, you know. Many women your age need a hearing aid. Have you seen a doctor?"

"I don't need to see a doctor! My ears are fine!"

"Then I really don't know what the problem is."

"The problem is that this… gift you have, isn't something you can teach. It's probably genetic."

"You think?"

"Of course!"

The two women stared at Harriet, who looked concerned, and so did Brutus.

"But, Gran," said Harriet. "If we can't teach humans to talk to us, this whole Baker Street Cats project is useless!"

"Yeah, if we don't have a human operator who can interpret the messages my soldiers send in," said Brutus, "the app won't work."

"Nonsense," said Gran. "We'll just have to find a way to make it work. Look, if they can put Jeff Bezos in space, how hard can it be to create an app that makes sense of what you're saying?"

"There's only one solution as I see it," said Scarlett.

"Which is?"

"That you and Marge and Odelia work around the clock to man the command center where all the information from the Baker Street Cats comes in, and work as dispatchers."

"I'm not going to spend the rest of my life as a dispatcher," said Gran. "No way."

"Well, if you want this to work, you'll have to."

"Marge can do it," said Harriet. "I mean, how many people go to the library nowadays?"

"Yeah, kids don't read books anymore," Brutus chimed in. "They all play computer games, or chat with their friends on WhatsApp or watch TikTok. They don't need books."

"He's right, you know," said Harriet. "Libraries are a thing of the past, Gran, so Marge should come on board, and become the world's first Baker Street Cats dispatcher."

"I very much doubt she'll want to do that," Gran grunted.

"Well, she'll have to, or otherwise this project will be a bust!"

"Odelia is going to have a baby," suddenly Dooley interjected, sounding gloomy.

All those present, except for Scarlett, regarded him with astonishment. Though the responses were markedly different: Gran looked elated, Harriet was frowning and didn't look happy, and Brutus looked pretty much indifferent.

"A baby!" Gran cried.

"What baby?" asked Scarlett.

"Odelia is pregnant!" Gran said.

"She's not pregnant," I said, hastening to put the record straight before the whole town was buzzing with news that wasn't news. "All she said was that she wants to start a family."

"So she's not pregnant?" asked Gran.

"No, she's not—at least not as far as I know."

"Oh," said Gran, her face sagging.

"So is she pregnant or isn't she pregnant?" asked Scarlett.

"I'm not sure," said Gran. "Dooley says she is, and Max says she isn't."

"Let's ask her," said Scarlett, closing her notebook, visibly relieved her lessons for the day were over. "Odelia!" she hollered, getting up. "Oh, Odelia!"

Odelia's head popped through the opening in the hedge. "Yes?"

"Is it true that you're pregnant?" asked Scarlett.

Odelia frowned. "Of course not—why do you ask?"

"Your cats seem to think so."

"Do they now?" said Odelia, cutting a curious glance in my direction.

I was shaking my head, but before I could deny the charge, Gran said, "It would be great if you were pregnant, honey. It's what we're all waiting for, you know."

"Frankly whether I'm pregnant or not is none of your

business, Gran," said Odelia, "or yours, for that matter, Scarlett."

"Well!" said Scarlett, taken aback.

"But for your information, I'm not pregnant, and even if I was, the first person I'd tell would be my husband." And with these words, she turned on her heel and disappeared again.

"She's pregnant," said Scarlett knowingly. "Only a pregnant woman would be so catty."

"She's not catty," said Gran. "Or is she?"

"Oh, she's catty all right. Did you see the way she was looking at me? Hormones."

"I'm not sure," said Gran. Then a keen look came into her eyes. "Let's ask Marge. If anyone knows, it'll be Marge."

"Marge!" Scarlett bellowed. "Marge, come here a minute, will you!"

Marge's head now popped through the kitchen window. "What?" she asked, looking a little harried. Libraries might be a thing of the past, but the library where Marge worked still seemed to give her plenty of work.

"Is it true that Odelia is pregnant?" asked Scarlett, not beating about the bush.

Marge frowned. "What?

"Pregnant," said Scarlett.

"We have it on good authority that you're going to be a grandmother soon," said Gran.

"And you a great-grandmother," Scarlett pointed out, causing a slight lessening of Gran's exuberance.

"Great-grandmother," she repeated. "Oh, my…"

"Oh, don't talk nonsense," said Marge. "If my daughter were pregnant, don't you think she would have told me?"

"So she's not pregnant?" asked Scarlett.

"Of course not."

"Huh!" said Scarlett, as Marge's head disappeared.

"Oh, I know," said Gran. "Let's ask Tex."

"Of course! If anyone knows, it's Odelia's doctor. Tex!" she screamed. "Oh, Texie!"

Tex's head came popping out of the upstairs bedroom window, where presumably he'd been engaged in admiring the portrait of his gnome, the pride of his collection. "What is it?" he asked. "Where is the fire?"

"No fire," said Scarlett. "Just that we heard that congratulations are in order."

"What congratulations?" asked Tex, looking puzzled.

"Oh, don't be coy, Tex. We know you're going to be a grandfather soon!"

Tex's face lit up. "I am? Oh, that's wonderful news."

"You mean you didn't know?" asked Scarlett.

"No, I didn't. This is news to me—but wonderful, absolutely wonderful."

"But you are your daughter's doctor, aren't you?"

"I'm not a gynecologist, Scarlett," said Tex.

"So you wouldn't know if she were pregnant?" Scarlett insisted.

"Not unless she told me," said Tex.

"Okay, Tex, go away," said Gran. "We don't need you anymore."

"Oh," said Tex, giving us a look of confusion, retracting his head again.

Just then, Chase came walking through the hedge, and gave us an all-encompassing smile. "Still working on those cat-talking skills, are you, Scarlett?" he said.

"Chase, you're the dad," said Scarlett, pouncing on the cop. "So when is the big day?"

"What big day?" asked Chase.

"When is your wife's due date?!" Scarlett insisted.

"Due date?"

"Babies, Chase!" said Gran. "When is the baby due?"

"Before you can have a due date, first you need to be

pregnant," the cop pointed out.

"Oh, don't keep us in suspense!" Gran snapped. "Is your wife pregnant or isn't she?"

Chase gave her a smile. "That's for me to know and for you to find out, isn't it?"

And with these cryptic words, he walked into the house.

"This family of yours is just terrible!" said Scarlett.

"Yeah, so secretive," Gran murmured.

And then, slowly, they both turned to me. And soon I found that Harriet, Brutus and Dooley were also staring at me.

"You're Odelia's top cat, Max," said Harriet.

"Yeah, if anyone knows her deepest darkest secrets, it's you," Brutus added.

"A baby is not a dark secret, Brutus," said Gran.

"No, I guess it's not," Brutus amended his statement.

"But you know, don't you, Max!" said Harriet.

"Look, you guys, I have no idea what goes on behind closed doors!" I said.

"Oh, but you do, Max—you always do," said Harriet.

"Yeah, you're a clever little detective, aren't you, Max?" said Brutus.

"If anyone knows, it's you, Max!" said Gran.

"And if he doesn't know now, he'll be able to find out, won't you, Max?" said Scarlett.

"But you guys!" I cried.

"You have to find out, Max," said Harriet.

"Yeah, our lives depend on it," Brutus chimed in.

"A baby is going to change everything, Max," said Dooley.

"As we all know: when babies come, cats have to go," Harriet added.

"Which means we'll have to go," said Brutus.

"No more sleeping at the foot of the bed," said Harriet.

"No more spending time lazing around the house," Brutus added.

"The good old days are over, Max," said Harriet.

"Yeah, it's bye-bye cats," said Gran.

"At least as long as that baby is an infant," Brutus pointed out. He turned to Harriet. "How long does it last, that infancy stage?"

"Oh, probably until the kid goes off to college?" said Harriet.

"College!" Dooley cried. "But that's… a very long time!"

"Okay, so it's a matter of life or death, Max," said Gran.

"You have to find out if Odelia is pregnant—now!" Harriet stressed.

"Oh, all right!" I said. "I will find out, I promise!"

Okay, so I finally caved. But what did you expect? It was indeed a matter of life or death for us cats! Harriet was right: when babies come, cats have to go! And I honestly didn't feel like going just yet. I was much too young to go! I really was!

CHAPTER 18

And so I found myself, sandwiched between Harriet and Brutus in the back of Gran's little red Peugeot, my two friends chattering excitedly about my 'mission' and discussing the pros and cons of the new baby arriving in our midst. Dooley was seated next to Brutus, having been muscled out of the center of things, and frankly I wasn't feeling all that sanguine with my new position as potential savior of the Poole cat contingent.

At least there was one silver lining about all of this: no longer were the Baker Street Cats the center of attention. The downside was that there was actual talk of sabotaging any potential arrival of the new baby in our midst!

"Babies are bad for business, Max, you have to accept that," said Harriet in hushed tones.

"What do you mean?" I asked.

"Well, as we all know, the moment a baby arrives, humans kick their cats to the curb."

"And we're talking the actual curb, Max," said Brutus.

"We'll have to live on the street," said Harriet. "Eat from dumpsters."

"We'll be living like Clarice," said Brutus. "And you know what that means."

"Rats and mice," Harriet added.

"They'll be all the food we'll have."

"Apart from the occasional leftovers."

"No more gourmet food for us, Max. No more delicious kibble. No more wet food pouches. No, the moment that baby arrives, the family will close ranks and they'll kick us all out—to live on the street like common mongrels!"

"So it's imperative that we come up with a plan of campaign," said Harriet.

"First," said Brutus, like the general that he imagined himself to be, "we need to make sure there really is a baby."

"Second," said Harriet, "if there is no baby, we need to make sure there won't be a baby."

"What?!" I cried, alarmed by this train of thought.

"Look, this is a matter of life or death, Max," said Harriet sternly.

"A question of it or us," said Brutus.

"But you guys!" I said.

"It's very simple, Max," said Harriet. "All you need to do is make sure that Odelia takes her pills."

"What pills?" asked Dooley.

"The anti-baby kind," Harriet snapped.

"They have anti-baby pills?"

"Of course they do. So you just make sure Odelia keeps taking her pills, and we're in the clear."

"And how do you propose I do that?" I asked.

"I don't know. Maybe you mix them in her corn flakes? Or put them in her coffee?"

"But Harriet!" I said. "I can't do that!"

"It does sound a little harsh when you put it like that, sexy legs," Brutus said.

"Yeah, I know," said Harriet. "I heard myself just now and it does sound harsh."

"Cruel."

"But essential for our survival!" Harriet cried.

"Maybe babies are not so bad," said Dooley.

"Dooley, how can you say that!" Harriet hissed.

"Most people seem to like them. And I'm sure they get good reviews on Yelp."

"You don't know what you're saying, Dooley," said Brutus, shaking his head.

"Oh, but I do. I've seen plenty of documentaries about babies. They're very nice to look at. Ten little toes, ten little fingers… And that baby fuzz on top of their little heads."

"Babies are a cat's natural enemy, Dooley," said Brutus, "and it's important we don't become soft and allow ourselves to be seduced by their innate cuteness."

"It's that cuteness that hides their essential dark nature!" said Harriet.

"That cuteness is nature's way of seducing us to the dark side."

"But they look like so much fun!" said Dooley.

"Don't be tempted, Dooley!" said Brutus.

"Yeah, don't be fooled, Dooley," said Harriet. "A baby is, for all intents and purposes, the worst thing that can happen to a cat. The absolute worst."

"Yes, this is war, Dooley. War against a vicious enemy!"

"And what do you do with an enemy, Dooley?" asked Harriet.

"Um… you negotiate a peace treaty?" Dooley suggested.

"No!" Brutus cried. "You attack! No mercy! And that goes for you, too, Max."

"It does?" I asked.

"Yes. This is the time to show what you're made of."

"It is?"

"Absolutely. It's either us... or it."

"Okay," I said, feeling a little queasy all of a sudden.

"If it's a boy we'll name it Frank," said Gran.

"No, let's name it Jack," said Scarlett.

"Let's put a pin in it for the moment," said Gran, who was in too good a mood to argue with her best friend. "And if it's a girl? Franky."

"Or Jacky," Scarlett suggested. "And of course I'll be the godmother."

"Of course," said Gran good-naturedly.

In fact they were so busy discussing possible names for the baby that they didn't seem to be paying all that much attention to potential criminals roaming our streets and engaging in all kinds of nefarious activities. But then suddenly a young man came running out of a house and right in front of the car! He was barefoot and only wearing a pair of boxers. The headlights of the Peugeot lit up his features, which were contorted in a look of sheer and utter panic. Maybe he'd seen a baby.

"Stop!" he cried as he waved his hands frantically. "Please, stop!"

And so Gran stopped the car and poked her head out of the window. "What do you think you're doing, Sonny Jim!" she yelled. "Jumping in front of my car like that."

"It's my friend!" the kid cried. "I think he's dead!"

"What friend? What are you talking about?"

"Todd," said the kid. "I think he drowned!"

CHAPTER 19

It was as the kid said: when we hurried out of the car and followed him around the back of the house, we came upon a pool, next to which a body was lying. Immediately Scarlett and Gran started CPR, but it was too late. It was clear that Todd Bond had been dead for some time.

"When did you find him?" asked Gran as Scarlett called the police.

"Just now," said the kid, who was seated on a pool lounger, hugging himself and rocking backward and forward, clearly in some kind of a state. "I'd gone to bed, and Todd had decided to stay up, saying there was something he needed to do. I woke up to go to the bathroom, and saw that the pool lights were still on—my parents like us to switch them off when we go to bed. And that's when I saw him. Floating in the pool. I dragged him out, and tried CPR, but it didn't work!"

"Looks like he was in that pool for a while," said Gran, studying the dead boy.

A young woman came out of the house, looking sleepy. "What's going on?" she asked. But then she saw the body of the teenager lying next to the pool, and a look of horror crept up her face. "Oh, my God, Todd!"

She moved forward, but Scarlett held her back. "I'm sorry, but there's nothing you can do," she said.

"What happened!" the girl cried, tears springing to her eyes.

"I don't know," said the kid. "I went to the bathroom ten minutes ago and saw him in the pool."

"Oh, my God!" the girl screamed, and looked beside herself with what could only be terrible grief.

"Who are you?" asked Gran, addressing the girl.

"She's my sister Layla," said the kid.

"And you are?"

"Scott," said the kid. "Scott Walcott."

"And you're a friend of Todd?"

The kid nodded. "Yeah, we've been friends forever."

"So what happened?"

Scott shrugged. "I don't know. He must have accidentally stumbled into the pool."

"And you didn't hear anything?"

"No, our bedrooms are on the other side of the house." He buried his head in his hands. "If I hadn't gone to the bathroom, we wouldn't have found him until tomorrow morning. He'd have been in that pool all night."

Sirens could be heard, and moments later the police arrived, and an ambulance. It was as we'd surmised, though: nothing could be done for Todd, and the doctor pronounced him dead at the scene, estimating that he'd probably been dead for over an hour.

Gran glanced at her watch. "It's two o'clock now. Which means he died around one. What time did you go to bed, Scott?"

Scott was rubbing his face, while Scarlett had taken his

sister inside, so she wouldn't have to be confronted with the turmoil that followed these terrible events.

"Um... must have been before midnight. Eleven thirty, eleven forty-five, I think."

Chase now arrived, followed by Odelia, and when Odelia saw the dead boy's body, she grimaced. "Todd Bond," she said immediately.

And as Gran brought Chase and Odelia up to date, Dooley and I, along with Brutus and Harriet, decided to head inside, and see if the Walcotts had any pets that could tell us what happened.

Unfortunately for us they didn't. No dogs, no cats—not even a goldfish.

"Odd," said Dooley as we headed up the stairs. "Most families have at least one pet."

"Yeah, not everybody likes pets," I said. All was quiet upstairs, as the activity was now focused outside and in the downstairs kitchen, where Scarlett had made Layla Walcott some hot tea to drink. We came upon what was presumably the bedroom of Scott, and saw that a second bed had been slept in. "Looks like Scott and Todd were bunking," I said as we studied the room, which was a big mess.

Nothing immediately drew our attention, though, and so we moved to the other rooms on the second floor: one was clearly a girl's bedroom, and a third room was the parents' room, which was neat and tidy, the bed not slept in.

"Looks like the parents aren't home," I said.

Which would explain why Todd was staying there and nobody knew about it.

"So Tilton Bond was right," said Dooley, "when he told Odelia that Todd was probably staying with a friend."

"Yeah, but that still begs the question: how did he drown?"

"Maybe he couldn't swim, and he got drunk and stumbled into the pool?" Dooley suggested. "It happens a lot."

"It does happen a lot," I agreed.

"About the baby, Max," said Dooley, giving me an anxious look. "What are you…"

"Trust me, Dooley, I'm not going to do anything to stop Odelia from having a baby. In fact I'm absolutely convinced that if Odelia and Chase do have a baby, they won't kick us out, like Harriet and Brutus seem to think, but will make other arrangements."

"What arrangements?"

"I don't know. Maybe we'll all have to go and stay with Gran for a while?"

"That wouldn't be so bad."

"No, it wouldn't." I gave my friend an encouraging smile. "I'm glad to see you're taking the news so well, Dooley."

And he was. Once upon a time he'd been the one to get all in a tizzy over the news that Odelia might be having a baby.

"If there's one thing I've learned, Max, it is that Odelia is very fond of us, and so is Chase, so I don't think she'd ever kick us out, whatever Harriet and Brutus think."

"No, you're absolutely right. They wouldn't kick us out. Baby or no baby. And for what it's worth—I don't think there even is a baby. Otherwise Odelia would have told us."

We had returned to the bedroom Scott had shared with Todd, and Dooley sighed. "Poor kid."

"And poor Rosa. Not only did she lose a husband, now she's losing a son."

Footsteps sounded on the stairs, and moments later Chase arrived, along with Odelia, and followed by Scott. Scott showed them the bedroom, and said, "Todd often stayed over, so when he called me and asked if he could spend the weekend, I figured his mom knew."

"He didn't mention that he hadn't told her?" Odelia asked.

"No, he didn't. Though he did look tense when he arrived."

"Tense, how?" asked Chase.

"Well, Todd has never been the life and soul of the party. He's always been this serious kid, you know. But now he was even more quiet than usual."

"Did he tell you why?"

"He said he'd had a fight with his stepdad. But that wasn't so unusual. Todd and his stepdad didn't get along very well."

"They often fought?"

"Yeah, they did. Todd didn't like it when his stepdad laid down the rules. He wouldn't accept that from a man who wasn't his dad."

"What did they fight about?" asked Chase.

"The usual," said Scott. "Todd wanted to go to a concert, and Tilton had told him he couldn't go since his grades weren't good enough. They had some kind of arrangement that when he was doing well in school, he could go out on the weekends, but not on a school night. But this concert was on a school night, so Todd had hoped to get special permission, just this once, but Tilton put his foot down, and said that he couldn't go."

"He wasn't doing well in school?"

"No, lately his grades had slipped."

"And why was that, do you know?"

"He seemed preoccupied."

"About what?"

"He didn't tell me. I asked, but he said it had something to do with his family."

"But he wouldn't say more?"

"No, he wouldn't. I just figured it was his stepdad."

"Those fights they had."

"Yeah. I was surprised that he was allowed to stay out all

weekend, though, especially since last weekend he'd been grounded."

"What for?"

"Bad grades, I thought. Both Tilton and Rosa were very strict about that kind of stuff."

"How did Todd end up in your pool, Scott?" asked Odelia.

"I don't know, I swear."

"Did you have a party?" asked Chase.

"No, absolutely not. We were going to have a party tomorrow night, and I'd already invited some friends, but tonight was just a regular night."

"What did you do?"

"Nothing special. We just hung out by the pool."

"How much did Todd have to drink?"

"Not much. A couple of beers, maybe. We cooked together, then had dinner out by the pool, then just hung out for a while." When he saw that Chase didn't believe him, he said, emphatically, "I'm telling the truth, sir. You can ask Layla. We just hung out and then we played some video games, watched some television, then went to bed."

"But not Todd."

"No, like I already told that old lady, he wanted to stay up, said he wasn't tired, and wanted to sit out by the pool for a while." He shrugged. "I just figured that he needed to clear his mind, you know—with everything that was going on between him and Tilton."

"Did you use any drugs, Scott?" asked Chase. "And remember that we will find out."

"No, drugs, sir." When Chase gave him a hard stare, he relented. "Maybe a little weed."

"So can you explain to me how Todd ended up dead in your pool, Scott?"

"I swear I don't know, sir."

"He was a good swimmer?"

"Yes, he was."

"Did he ever talk to you about his real dad?" asked Odelia, trying a different tack.

"His real dad? No, ma'am, he didn't. Well, just to say that he was out of the picture, and had been a real scumbag for leaving him and his mom like that."

"But he never told you he was in touch with him or anything?"

"Or that he wanted to look him up?" asked Chase.

"No, sir. He never mentioned anything like that. Not to me, anyway." He hesitated, then shook his head decidedly. "When I went to bed he was fine—just fine. So I have absolutely no idea what happened. Not a clue."

CHAPTER 20

Even though it was the middle of the night, we made our way to the Bonds, to inform them of the death of their son. It was a task that couldn't be put off until the morning. It was also a task that no one likes to perform, but it had to be done, and so we rode in the car with Chase and Odelia and stood by as they rang the doorbell and waited patiently until Mrs. Bond and her husband appeared, looking sleepy and not a little bit rattled.

When the police show up on your doorstep in the middle of the night, it is never a good sign. And when you've just informed them of your son going missing, even worse.

I could tell from Rosa's expression that she already knew that Chase and Odelia weren't harbingers of glad tidings, and already Tilton Bond was supporting her as Chase said, in somber tones, "I'm sorry to have to tell you that we've found Todd, Mrs. Bond."

"Oh, no," said Rosa, clasping a hand to her mouth. "He's not... dead?"

"I'm afraid he is."

"No!" she cried, then wordlessly opened and closed her

lips, even as she staggered back. We all moved inside, and there, seated on the cozy couch in the living room, Odelia and Chase took turns to inform the parents of the boy that Todd had died that night.

"I knew he hadn't left for Mexico," said Tilton softly. "I should have gone looking for him, instead of relying on his good sense to come home again when he felt he should."

"But how?" asked Rosa. "How did he die? He was such a good swimmer."

"The investigation will have to bear that out," said Chase.

Todd's sister Aisha, awakened by the voices, now also came down and joined us. When she was informed, by her stepdad, of what had happened to her brother, she went very quiet and very, very pale. She just sat there, looking thoroughly shocked, and I think it was understandable that Odelia and Chase left soon after. There was no point asking a lot of questions now, coming so soon upon the terrible tragedy. Todd's parents and his sister needed to process what had happened, and maybe in the morning questions could be asked, and the investigation begun in earnest as to what had happened to the boy.

For now, at least, it was time for us to go home, and get some rest.

I still couldn't help, though, to ask, while we were driving home, "Odelia? Is it true that you're having a baby soon?"

In spite of the tragic events, Odelia smiled. "I knew you were going to ask that, Max. And no, for your information, I'm not pregnant. So you can put all your concerns to rest, and also those of Gran and Scarlett and the others. If or when the time comes, I promise you'll be the first to know, all right?"

"Pregnant?" asked Chase.

"Somehow the cats have gotten it into their nut that I'm having a baby," said Odelia. "Don't ask me how."

"But you said so," said Dooley. "When Rosa asked if you were thinking about starting a family, you said, 'Oh, absolutely.'"

"And I wasn't lying, Dooley," said Odelia. "But that doesn't mean we're starting a family right now."

"Oh," said Dooley, and shared a look of relief with me.

"Look, Harriet and Brutus are going to ask you a lot of questions," I told my human. "In fact they even told me to do anything that lies in my power to prevent this baby from joining our family, and I think you should probably know that they're extremely worried."

"And why is that, pray tell?" asked Odelia, that look of amusement still playing about her lips.

"Because they think you'll kick us out the moment the baby is born," said Dooley.

"Oh, please," said Odelia. "You know I would never do that, don't you?"

"But cats and babies don't mix, Odelia," said Dooley. "Everybody knows that."

"But you're not like other cats, are you?"

"We're not?"

"No, you're very special kitties, and I'm sure that if I had a baby, you would never think of harming a hair on that baby's head, now would you?"

"No, of course not," said Dooley, cutting me a look of concern.

"Harriet and Brutus did seem very anxious," I said. "And I do mean very, very anxious."

"I'll have to have a talk with them," said Odelia. "But I can promise you right now, that when Chase and I decide to have a baby…"

"Which will be soon, if it's up to me," Chase added with a slight grin.

"Very soon," Odelia confirmed, sharing a knowing glance

with her husband, "you can rest assured that you won't be kicked out. But you have to promise me to take good care of this baby, all right?"

"Of course," I said warmly.

"We will take very good care of the baby, Odelia," Dooley intoned.

"But you will talk to Harriet and Brutus, though, won't you?" I asked once more.

"Oh, you can bet on it," she said, and I had the distinct impression that a few home truths were about to be dispensed to that fearsome twosome.

CHAPTER 21

The next morning, we found ourselves the guests of the Bond family once again. Tilton and Rosa sat where they'd sat last night, and so did Aisha.

"I don't understand," said Rosa, and it was clear she hadn't had any sleep, and neither had Tilton. "Todd was such a good swimmer." She was holding a picture of her boy, probably aged twelve at the time, holding up a medal which he'd won in a swimming competition. She showed it to Odelia and Chase, to prove that her boy couldn't have possibly drowned.

Tilton had placed a comforting arm around his wife's shoulder, but he, too, looked badly affected by what happened.

"Do you think he might have… done this to himself?" asked Odelia.

Rosa looked up. "You mean did he kill himself?"

"He would never do that," said Aisha. "Never."

"He did seem unhappy lately," said Tilton.

"You had an argument with Todd before he ran off?" asked Chase.

"I did, yes," said Tilton.

"What was the argument about?"

"The usual," said Tilton. "His grades had been slipping lately, and I told him that he needed to focus more on school and less on some of the extracurricular activities he liked to get involved in."

"Like what?"

"Partying with his friends, obviously, but also some concert he wanted to go to."

"Stage Patrol," said Aisha with a faint smile. "He just loved that band."

"Since it was a school night, we felt he shouldn't go," Rosa explained.

"Especially since his grades weren't good," Tilton specified. "I told him that if he applied himself more, that maybe we could allow him to go to concerts and whatever, but as long as his grades kept slipping, first he needed to address that."

"He felt you were being too strict with him," said Aisha softly.

"But we were only doing it for his own good," Rosa said.

"I know, Mom, and I think Todd did, too."

"Do you have any idea why he decided to stay with Scott, Aisha?" asked Odelia.

Aisha shrugged, but didn't look up.

"Aisha?" asked Rosa, alarmed.

"Well, the thing is that Todd had a girlfriend," said Aisha, "and I think he wanted to spend more time with her than with us."

"Girlfriend?" asked Rosa, who looked greatly surprised by this. "What girlfriend? He never said anything about a girlfriend."

"Well, he wouldn't, would he?" said Aisha. "You would just have told him he couldn't see her anymore, not until his grades improved."

"Who was the girlfriend, Aisha?" asked Chase gently.

"Scott's sister. Layla," said Aisha, her eyes still fixed on the carpet.

Odelia and Chase shared a look of surprise, and so did Rosa and Tilton.

"Scott didn't approve, though, so Todd and Layla tried to keep a low profile. Which is why they hadn't told anybody, not even me. I caught him texting her one night, so that's how I found out. I confronted him about the text, and so he told me the whole story."

"Scott didn't approve of his sister dating his best friend?" asked Odelia.

"No, he thought it was creepy that his sister would get involved with Todd." She shrugged. "Don't ask me why. I thought he would have been happy, but Todd said he freaked out. So they told him they'd broken up, just to make him calm down."

"But they hadn't?"

Aisha shook her head. "As far as I know they were still seeing each other, only they were making sure that Scott didn't find out this time."

"That must have been tough on Todd," said Odelia.

"Yeah, well, he seemed to handle it just fine."

"Would you happen to know where Todd's phone is, Aisha?" asked Chase.

Rosa was surprised. "He didn't have it with him?"

"We haven't found it yet," said Odelia.

"Maybe it's in his room," Tilton suggested.

Aisha got up. "I'll go check," she said, and quickly disappeared.

"Todd never told me he was dating Layla Walcott," said Rosa. She looked to her husband. "Why didn't he tell us, Tilton?"

"Because he was a teenager, honey. Boys Todd's age don't confide in their parents, especially about the girls they like."

"But Todd never kept any secrets from me before—he knew he could tell me everything. Always."

"I think it's not unusual for kids not to tell their mother about the girl they're dating, Rosa," Odelia said softly.

She nodded, tears trickling down her cheeks. "He could have told me. He knew I would have listened."

Aisha entered the room again and shook her head. "It's not in his room. I checked."

"I'm sure we'll find it," said Chase.

CHAPTER 22

I would like to say that Odelia and Chase went full steam ahead with their investigation into Todd's death, but they both looked pretty bushed, and that was only to be expected. It had of course been a long night for them, and they hadn't gotten a lot of sleep. Still, they had a job to do, so onward they went, with me and Dooley in tow.

Harriet and Brutus had opted to stay home and engage in one more valiant attempt to teach Scarlett the finer points of the feline language. Though I could see that their initial excitement had already waned to a great degree. I think the experience had instilled in them a newfound respect for the teaching profession, though. Imagine how hard it must be to teach a group of young ruffians the finer points of algebra, math, or grammar?

I was glad I was out and about, instead of being cooped up inside, acting as a private tutor to Scarlett. And so when we arrived at the house where Todd Bond had drowned last night, I was ready for any fate, and to discover what could possibly have gone wrong that this young man had met such an untimely death.

In the drive over, Chase and Odelia had offered all kinds of theories as to what could have happened, but none of them seemed satisfactory in explaining the tragedy that had befallen the Bond family.

The first person we talked to was Layla Walcott. The girl still looked properly impressed by what had happened, but she was composed enough to answer our questions with dignity and honesty—or at least I hoped she was. One never knows if people are telling the truth, of course, and a feline lie detector, unfortunately, I am not.

Still, there is a great deal one can glean from facial expressions, mannerisms and tone of voice, and Layla struck me as fundamentally cooperative.

"Yes, Todd and I dated for a while," she admitted. "But we broke up about a month ago, which made his staying here pretty awkward, I can tell you."

We were sitting out on the terrace, even though this was the place where the tragedy had occurred. But the crime scene people had done their jobs, and nothing about the swimming pool area gave any indication of the drama that had taken place there the night before.

"You broke up?" asked Odelia.

Layla nodded. She was dressed in a light summer dress, and if she was bowled over by the death of her former boyfriend she didn't look it. No Romeo and Juliet scenario here. "Yeah, we both agreed it was too weird, with my brother being his best friend."

"Your brother knew about it?"

"He did, and he didn't like it one bit. In fact he was the one who told me to break it off."

"And you did."

"Not because he said so, but yeah, we felt that the relationship had run its course."

"How long had you been an item?" asked Chase, jotting down the odd note in his little notebook.

"Um, about four months," said Layla.

"That's not long," said Dooley.

"At her age four months is an eternity, Dooley," I said.

"Did you notice anything unusual about Todd last night, or the last couple of days?" asked Odelia.

Layla frowned and rubbed her nose. "Yeah, actually I did. He seemed moody, and distracted. His grades had been dropping, too, which was weird, since he'd always been an ace at school. And now all of a sudden he was neglecting his studies."

"Did you talk about it with him?"

"No, not really. Things had been a little weird between us, ever since we... you know."

Odelia nodded. "So he didn't confide in you about what was troubling him?"

"No, but I think it probably had something to do with his dad."

"His dad?"

"Yeah, he didn't get along with his dad, or at least that's what he told me when we were still seeing each other. Said Tilton was very strict, and wouldn't let him go out if his grades weren't good enough."

"And he didn't like that."

"No, especially since Tilton wasn't even his real dad."

"Did he ever talk about his real dad?" asked Chase.

Layla shook her head. "Only that he met another woman and had left them. Which had been hard on his family."

"Did he say anything about wanting to go look for his real dad?"

"I don't think so. But like I said, we hadn't really talked since the split."

"Was he seeing some other girl maybe?" asked Odelia.

"I doubt it. I would have heard. But maybe you should ask my brother. He and Todd have always been really close. Maybe he'll tell you more."

Contrary to his sister, Scott seemed reluctant to divulge his best friend's secrets to us. He looked a little sullen as he sat there, his hair hanging in front of his eyes, and more lying in his chair than sitting. "I don't know anything, all right?" he said in response to a question about a potential new girlfriend.

"So he didn't confide in you about what was going on in his life?" asked Chase.

Todd shrugged. He glanced to the pool, then looked away again. "My parents called. They've decided to cut their trip short."

"Where did they go?"

"The Bahamas. They go there every year. They sounded pretty upset when I told them what happened."

"It's not your fault, Scott," said Odelia.

He shrugged. "Try telling them that."

"So let's go over this again, shall we?" said Chase.

Scott sighed deeply and swept his blond fringe from his eyes. "Look, I already told you everything I know: I went to bed, Layla had already gone up earlier, and Todd said he was going to stay up for a while. He said he needed to think."

"Think about what?"

"I don't know. He didn't want to tell me what was going on. But it had something to do with his family."

"Did he mention getting in touch with his real dad?" asked Chase.

Scott hesitated. "Not last night. But he said something about it last week."

"What did he say?"

"Just that he wanted to find his dad, and ask him why he left."

"Did he mention arranging a meeting? Traveling to see him?"

"I don't think so. But something was definitely going on. He kept looking at his phone all evening, as if he was expecting a call or something, or a message."

"Maybe he was just worried that his mom would come look for him," Odelia suggested.

"Yeah, could be. Though they can't have been too worried, cause last time he went missing, he also spent the weekend with us."

"What did your parents have to say about that?" asked Odelia.

"They weren't happy, I can tell you that. Todd's mom and dad came over and had a talk with my mom and dad, and of course they blamed the whole thing on me. They ended up grounding me for two weeks, and taking away my internet privileges for a whole month."

"And still when Todd dropped by you didn't tell him to go home?"

"He was my friend. I couldn't tell him to take a hike, now could I? Besides, he didn't tell me he'd run away from home. He said he'd told his mom where he was."

"And you believed him?"

"Of course. I didn't have a reason not to believe him."

"Do you have any idea what happened to Todd's phone, Scott?"

Scott frowned. "Didn't he have it on him?"

"No, he didn't. And we've looked everywhere and can't find it."

"Have you tried Find My Phone?"

"His laptop seems to have gone missing, too," said Chase.

"That's weird. He had it with him when he arrived. Are you sure it's not upstairs?"

"No, we've checked."

Scott's frown was still firmly in place when Odelia asked the next question: "We understand from your sister that she and Todd were dating for a while?"

He grimaced. "Yeah, talk about a match made in hell."

"Why do you say that?"

"Cause they weren't good for each other."

"They weren't?"

"Absolutely not. Todd wasn't a flashy kid. He wasn't into outward appearances and trying to look good. And that's exactly the kind of guys Layla is into: the jocks, the big, flashy guys who are all about what clothes they wear, and what their hair looks like."

"And Todd wasn't like that."

"No way. He hated that kind of stuff, and so do I."

"How did you feel about your sister dating your best friend, Scott?" asked Chase.

"I didn't like it. And I told him."

"But he wouldn't listen?"

"It wasn't like that. He knew that Layla wasn't the girl for him, only…" He hesitated.

"Only what, Scott?"

"Only Layla can be persistent, and she had developed this obsession with Todd, and wouldn't let go."

"She wouldn't?"

"She's like that: once she's got her mind set on something —or someone—she won't let go. It's sick." He seemed to realize what he was saying, because suddenly he sobered and said, "Please don't take this the wrong way. Layla would never hurt Todd. Never. She really liked him, and he liked her, just… they weren't for each other, see?"

"I think I understand," said Odelia.

"Layla tells us that she and Todd broke up?" said Chase.

Scott nodded. "Yeah, they did."

"Who broke up with whom?"

"It was a mutual decision."

"So no hard feelings from either side?"

"No, they were both fine with it."

"And you? You were probably relieved?"

The kid rolled his eyes. "It wasn't like that."

"But you didn't shed any tears when they announced it was over, right?"

"Not exactly. Look, is this going to take much longer? It's just that I need to get the house cleaned up before my parents arrive."

"When are they due back?"

"Soon!"

Chase got up, and so did Odelia. "Then I guess we better leave you to it."

Chase glanced across the pool, and pointed to the back of the garden. "Who lives over there, do you know?"

"Um, Mr. Durain."

I noticed how a window of the neighboring house looked out over the Walcott backyard. With any luck, that window was a bedroom window, and Mr. Durain was a light sleeper and a nosy parker and could tell us what happened last night.

CHAPTER 23

Mr. Lionel Durain proved to be a very nice old man, who was more than willing to assist us in our inquiries. He seemed eager to help us in any way he could.

"I heard all about it," he said by way of greeting when we turned up on his doorstep unannounced. "Some neighborhood kid that drowned, isn't that right?"

"How did you hear about it, Mr. Durain?" asked Chase as we stepped into the man's living room.

He was still dressed in his morning robe, and judging from the way his wavy gray hair was pointing in every direction, he hadn't yet enjoyed the benefit of a shower or bath.

"Oh, well, this is a close-knit community, detective, in spite of what you might think," said the man as he offered Odelia and Chase a seat on a creaky old couch. "We still talk to each other here, contrary to some other neighborhoods. It was actually Mrs. Taggart who told me. She runs the neighborhood committee, you see, of which I am a proud member."

"The neighborhood committee? Is that like a neighborhood watch?" asked Odelia.

"Oh, no, not at all. The purpose of the committee is not to increase safety, or to patrol the neighborhood, but to increase neighborliness—improve the social fabric of our small community, if you will. We organize barbecues in the summer, a neighborhood fête, a big Christmas do in the winter. Most neighborhoods nowadays are what they call bedroom communities. People come home from work, roll down the shutters, and camp out in front of the television for the rest of the evening. Next day they rise early, leave for work—rinse and repeat. You don't see them out and about. They might as well be invisible. But not here—oh, no. We make sure that neighbors still know each other by their first name."

"So did you notice anything unusual last night, Mr. Durain?" asked Chase. He pointed in the direction of the stairs. "We happened to notice how one of your upstairs windows oversees the Walcott backyard."

"So we were hoping you might have seen what happened," Odelia supplied.

"Unfortunately, no," said Mr. Durain. "Thought I did hear some strange noises during the night."

"What noises?" asked Odelia, perking up after she'd sagged a little when realizing that Chase's hunch wasn't going to play out.

"I'm a very light sleeper, you see, and every time the Walcotts go away on holiday, those kids like to organize parties for their friends. I've complained about it many times, but nobody seems to care. Let kids be kids, they say. But I have a right to sleep, don't I?"

"And last night there was such a party?"

"Not last night. The night before last. Last night they had a quiet evening at home for a change. I don't mind telling you that I was relieved, and decided to take advantage of the opportunity to go to bed early—take an advance on tonight, when I was pretty sure they'd be inviting all of their friends over again. Only I was woken up by someone shouting."

"Shouting?"

"Yes, I can't be sure, since I had been sleeping. And I use earplugs at all times. But I could have sworn I heard shouting. And splashing."

"Splashing?" asked Chase, exchanging a meaningful glance with Odelia.

"Yes. As if someone had stumbled into the pool and was splashing about and shouting. I sat up for a moment, listening intently, but the splashing stopped, and so did the shouting. So then I went back to sleep and didn't think anything more of it, until Mrs. Taggart arrived this morning and gave me the bad news. I immediately thought of what I heard, and I was actually just thinking about phoning the police when you arrived—very conveniently, I might add." He gave us a beaming smile, glad to be of assistance.

"Do you have any idea what time this was, sir?" asked Odelia.

"Well…" He thought for a moment. Then his face lit up. "Yes, actually I do. I'd gone to the bathroom not long before, and I don't think I'd been asleep long. You see, when you get to be my age, frequent visits to the bathroom are a given." He gave Chase a wink. "You're too young, my friend, but wait till you're a little older. You'll either want to install a toilet upstairs, or move into an apartment. Navigating a staircase in the middle of the night is the best recipe for breaking your neck." He frowned. "Now where was I? Oh, that's right. I'd gone to the bathroom, had settled in again, and that's when I woke up from that splashing and shouting. And when I was in the bathroom, I'd picked up my Kindle to do a bit of light reading—it sometimes takes a while before… you know, the river starts flowing, shall we say. So I like to have my Kindle to do some reading while I wait for those bodily functions to start working like they're supposed to—if you see what I mean."

"He takes an awfully long time to get to the point, Max," said Dooley.

"He does," I agreed.

"It's not just his bodily functions that are delayed, it's the rest of him, too."

"Be patient, Dooley. He's bound to get to the point... at some point."

"I'm reading an Agatha Christie book, by the way," said Mr. Durain. "Have you read Agatha Christie?"

"Yes, I have," said Odelia with an indulgent smile, as Chase's jaw was working feverishly. The cop clearly didn't have as much patience as Odelia had.

"I'm reading through her entire oeuvre right now, in chronological order. I always find that the best way to sample a beloved author is to read through their entire oeuvre in chronological order." He frowned again. "Now where was I?"

"You had just gone to the bathroom and you were waiting for... things to get going," said Chase helpfully.

"Oh, that's right. Well, at my age, things sometimes take their sweet time to get going, you see."

"Yes, I see," said Chase through gritted teeth.

"So as I was saying, I'd grabbed my Kindle, and out of habit I like to check what time it is, just to know if it's the middle of the night or closer to the morning. Just to know how much longer I can spend in the arms of Morpheus."

"Morpheus?" asked Dooley. "Is she Mr. Durain's wife?"

"It's an expression," I said. "Morpheus is the Greek god of dreams."

"What time was it?" asked Chase, his pencil poised over his notepad.

"One o'clock," said Mr. Durain. "On the dot."

"So those shouts and that splashing..." said Odelia

"Must have come on the heels of that."

"Did you spend a long time reading?" asked Odelia.

"Oh, no, not long. Lately I've been able to go much quicker. My doctor has given me some new tablets, you see. Something entirely new and revolutionary—or so he claims. Doctors are always saying that, of course. Though I have to admit that he seems to have hit on something good this time. These tablets are designed to encourage my prostate to release its usual death grip on my urinary tract. And I must say it seems to work a charm. It used to take me ten minutes to do my business and now sometimes I can get away with just under five. Which is an enormous ego boost, I can tell you." He gave me and Dooley a cheeky wink, and I gave him a wink in return, though I very much doubt he noticed.

"When you're old, you learn to savor the simple things in life, don't you, Max?" asked Dooley.

"Yes, you do, Dooley," I said.

"Like how long it takes you to go tinkle."

"So I'd say that the kid who fell into the pool must have done so around one fifteen," said Mr. Durain, keen to dot those I's and cross those t's.

"Thank you very much, Mr. Durain," said Odelia.

"Yes, you've been a great help," said Chase, though for some reason he couldn't make it sound as if he actually meant it. Ex-NYPD, you know. They're used to living life in the fast lane, and unfortunately for him, life in Hampton Cove is lived in the extremely slow lane.

CHAPTER 24

Once again we were in Uncle Alec's office, with Chase and Odelia reporting on their progress—or lack thereof—in the case of the drowned young man.

"So time of death seems to be around one fifteen in the morning," Odelia said in conclusion, as they recounted their recent encounter with the very helpful Mr. Durain. "Which jibes with what the doctor who was called to the scene said last night."

"And I just received Abe's preliminary report," said Uncle Alec, putting on his reading glasses and squinting at his computer screen. "Looks like a simple case of drowning. A modest amount of alcohol in the boy's system, traces of marijuana, but apart from that, nothing to indicate foul play. No signs of a struggle, no bruises or scratches on his body."

"So he simply... drowned?" asked Odelia.

"That seems to be the gist of it."

"But how can a perfectly healthy teenager simply drown?" asked our human.

"It happens, honey," said Uncle Alec, removing his reading glasses and placing them on top of his head, where presumably he'd soon forget about their existence and start groping around his desk in search of them.

"So he had too much to drink, went for a midnight swim and drowned?" asked Chase.

"That's about the gist of it. The young man smoked some weed with his friends, drank a couple of glasses, and when he went into the pool, the influence of the alcohol and the weed made him drowsy and caused him to lose his footing and so he went under and didn't come up. Happens more often than you think."

"It's possible he wasn't used to drinking," Chase suggested.

"But what about the scream?" asked Odelia.

"The scream?" asked Uncle Alec.

"The scream Mr. Durain heard."

Uncle Alec shrugged. "It's possible that he came up for air once, and realized he was in trouble. And then he went under a second time, a third time, and that was it. Game over. I'm sure he didn't suffer too much—the effect of the alcohol and the dope will have acted like a tranquilizer, causing his natural survival instincts to be dulled."

"I don't know, Uncle Alec," said Odelia, shaking her head. It was clear she wasn't satisfied with this explanation. "What about his phone that's gone missing, or his laptop?"

"I'm sure they'll turn up," said the Chief.

"We've asked Scott Walcott about it, and Layla, but they say they have no idea where Todd's phone or laptop could be," said Chase.

"So maybe he left them at home?"

"His mom or dad have no idea either," said Odelia. "Or his sister."

"Look, it's kids," said Uncle Alec. "They lose their phones all the time. You'll probably find it under his bed, or in the bushes where he dropped it."

"That entire backyard was searched by the forensics team, and they haven't found it," said Odelia. "We searched his room—both at home and at the Walcotts—and nothing."

Uncle Alec shrugged. He didn't seem to think this was such a big deal.

"I think we need to look into this case a little deeper," said Odelia.

"And I think this is a clear case of death by accidental drowning, and that's how I'm calling it," said the Chief stubbornly.

"What about Layla Walcott?" asked Odelia.

"What about her?"

"She dated Todd Bond, and said they split amicably—a mutual decision. But Scott said that his sister was obsessed with Todd."

"So now you think this Layla killed Todd, is that it?" asked the Chief, rubbing his eyes.

"It's a possibility," said Odelia. "A possibility I would like to dig into. Or maybe they were still seeing each other, in spite of their promise to Scott that they'd broken up, only Scott caught them kissing, and flew into a rage and—"

"Killed his best friend? We would have found something on the body to support that theory, Odelia," said Uncle Alec. "And there was nothing. No signs of a struggle or a fight."

"Well, I don't think—"

"Look, this case is closed, all right? I've called it. Now if you could please return to Josslyn Aldridge? We still haven't found her attacker, and frankly I'm starting to worry that we never will."

"But Uncle Alec…"

"Look, there's nothing here to indicate that Todd Bond's death wasn't an accident—nothing." He was tapping his desk and looking very stern and strict all of a sudden, and it was clear who was laying down the law in this town, and it wasn't Odelia or Chase.

"Yes, Chief," said Odelia.

"So Josslyn Aldridge. I can't emphasize enough how crucial the time element is in this case. Most likely she was attacked by an opportunistic bag snatcher, and it's imperative we find this guy before he skips town—if he hasn't already."

"The potential witness still hasn't come forward, Chief," said Chase.

"So we launch another appeal. We have to find this person. Charlene—Mayor Butterwick is feeling the pressure. The tourist board isn't happy with this kind of publicity. Robbery and murder isn't the best way to put this town on the map. And also the chairman of the chamber of commerce is putting pressure on the council to make this go away as quickly as possible, so the sooner we lay this case to rest the better. Oh, and also, Josslyn's sister arrived, and she would like to talk to the detective in charge."

"Josslyn's sister?" asked Chase.

"Yes, a…" He groped in vain for his glasses, until Odelia pointed out they were on top of his head, then consulted his written notes. "Leonora Ledger. She's here to arrange for the body of her sister to be flown back to Ohio, and also to find out why we still haven't caught the person responsible for her sister's death. So you talk to her, all right? Now."

"Yes, Chief," said Odelia and Chase in unison.

"Now get lost—and get me some results!"

CHAPTER 25

"Uncle Alec doesn't seem to believe that Todd Bond was murdered, does he, Max?" said Dooley.

"That's because the police have to follow the evidence, Dooley," I said, "and the evidence seems to indicate that the young man's death was an unfortunate accident."

"What do you think, Max? Do you think it was an accident?"

"I'm not sure," I said, and I wasn't lying. I still had my doubts, to be honest.

"But if he was killed, who could have done it?"

"Well, as far as I can tell, the most likely suspects are Scott or Layla," I said, "though to be sure we would need to investigate further. Ask Todd's friends—talk to Scott and Layla's parents—maybe interview other neighbors who might have heard something or seen something."

"But if the investigation is closed, that won't happen, right?"

"Unless Odelia decides to ignore her uncle's decision and continue the investigation in her own time."

But at that moment Odelia and Chase were too busy

conducting a different investigation. We were in the lobby of the Star Hotel, waiting for Josslyn Aldridge's sister to arrive to talk to us. Moments later the elevator dinged and two middle-aged ladies walked out. Odelia and Chase got up to greet them. Presumably these were Josslyn's sister and Josslyn's friend, the one with whom she'd come on this vacation. Sadly enough a vacation that had ended in tragedy.

"Let's sit outside," Odelia suggested, and escorted both women to the outside dining area, where we could talk undisturbed.

Josslyn's sister looked like her, only a few years older. She was a gray-haired woman of sizable proportions, and had to be supported by Josslyn's friend, whose name was Sadie Yentis. Sadie was about Josslyn's age, I would have guessed, which meant she was in her late fifties, early sixties. She was a round-faced, cheerful-looking woman with a frizzy mass of gray curly hair and large thick-framed glasses.

"So what can you tell us about the investigation?" asked Leonora. "Have you caught the man responsible for my sister's murder?"

"I'm afraid not," said Chase.

"But you were on TV," said Sadie. "I saw you. Has no one come forward?"

"We did receive several phone calls," said Chase, "but nothing helpful so far."

Leonora shook her head. "It's so sad. My sister was so looking forward to her retirement, when she finally could do all the things she'd been planning."

"We were going on a cruise next month," Sadie revealed. "We'd been saving for years."

"I'd go with you, but unfortunately my health won't allow it," said Leonora.

"These are the hardest cases to solve," said Odelia. "Because it's almost always a crime of opportunity. A bag snatcher sees an opportunity to target a potential victim and he strikes, then removes himself from the scene as soon as possible."

"It's often gangs, isn't it?" said Leonora. "Or at least that's what I read. Gangs of thieves moving from town to town and stealing from tourists." She shook her head. "Josslyn was simply at the wrong place at the wrong time. She's never had much luck in her life, I'm sorry to say."

"What makes you say that?" asked Odelia.

"Well, for one thing she never found a husband."

"She was in love once," Sadie said. "At least that's what she told me."

"It wouldn't surprise me if she was," said Leonora. "Josslyn was a hopeless romantic, always falling in love with men who were absolutely unsuitable—or even remotely interested in her. Unrequited love—the phrase must have been coined for her."

"She was very cheerful, though," said Sadie. "Happy to finally do what she wanted to do—go where she wanted to go."

"And then suddenly this…" Leonora fixed Odelia with a hopeful look. "Please tell me that you'll do everything that is in your power to catch this maniac. I simply cannot accept that my sister's death will be forgotten, the beast who killed her allowed to walk free."

"I can promise you that we are doing everything to find this person," said Odelia, placing her hand on the woman's arm in a gesture of reassurance.

"Oh, dear, oh, dear. I still can't believe that no one saw what happened."

"Don't you have cameras set up along the boardwalk?" asked Sadie.

"We do, but not at that particular spot," said Chase.

"Bad luck," said Leonora. "The story of Josslyn's life."

"Isn't there anything we can do, Max?" asked Dooley. "Look at how sad Josslyn's sister is, and her friend."

"It's as Chase explained, Dooley," I said. "These kinds of crimes are very hard to solve: oftentimes it's gangs moving from town to town during the tourist season. They probably left the area immediately after learning that Josslyn died as a consequence of the attack."

"Maybe we can talk to some of the dogs belonging to tourists walking along the boardwalk that night?"

"We could," I said dubiously. "But it would still be like looking for a needle in a haystack. Thousands of people pass along this boardwalk on any given day, and to find the one person who saw something will be very hard indeed." Besides, if no witnesses had come forward now, the likelihood that anyone saw something was very small. "No, I think we have to accept that here is a crime that might never be solved."

"But you have to solve it, Max," said Dooley. "You and that big beautiful brain of yours."

I gave him a small smile. "Even a big brain is no match for the thieves and pickpockets of this world, Dooley. Only diligent patrolling along the boardwalk can prevent that kind of crime, and I'm afraid that's not up to us, but up to Uncle Alec and his police force."

CHAPTER 26

That night, friends of Todd Bond had decided to organize a wake for their unfortunate friend. The place of the wake: the Walcotts. Apparently Scott and Layla's parents, even though they had returned from the Bahamas, had offered their house as a venue to organize the wake, and I thought this was very nice of them.

Odelia and Chase had decided to go, but had of course not been invited. The only reason they even knew about the wake was because Rosa had told Odelia. Our human, not satisfied with Uncle Alec's decision to close the case, had decided to keep on investigating, in her own time, and when Rosa phoned her about the wake, had decided to go.

And so Dooley and I found ourselves hiding in the bushes lining the backyard of the Walcott house, while Odelia and Chase were staking out the front, seated in their car, and making sure they clocked everyone coming and going, taking pictures of all participants.

I wasn't sure what they hoped to accomplish, but maybe it was a good idea to get a picture of the social circle Todd Bond had moved in.

"So Odelia still thinks it was foul play, does she?" asked Dooley, who was lying next to me on the cool grass.

"Yeah, she does," I said.

"I think so, too, Max. I don't think a kid like Todd would simply drown like that."

"It does all sound very suspicious," I agreed.

"I think Scott killed his friend. I think he was upset that his best friend was still dating his sister, and they got into an argument and he accidentally killed him."

"It is a possibility."

"It's not the kind of crime a girl would commit, is it, Max?"

"Girls are capable of murder, Dooley, not just boys."

"I know, but Layla seems like such a sweet girl."

We looked over to where Layla Walcott sat nursing a soda. She looked sad, and wasn't really talking much to anyone. Then again, this wasn't a party, this was a wake, and the atmosphere was appropriately subdued as a consequence. Scott and Layla's parents were there, serving drinks. They'd taken the precaution to close up the pool, covering it up with a large blue tarpaulin. It seemed like the safest and most respectful thing to do.

Rosa and Tilton Bond were also there, and stood chatting with Scott and Layla's folks. Scott himself was checking some notes he had in his hand, and I think he was going to read something he'd written, presumably saying a couple of words about his best friend.

Just then, Aisha Bond suddenly walked up to Layla Walcott, and threw a glass of orange juice into the girl's face! Immediately voices were raised, and a good deal of shouting ensued, and if both sets of parents hadn't kept the girls apart, I think hair-pulling and an actual physical altercation would have been in the cards as well. As it was, though, Aisha stomped off on a huff, ignoring her mother's shouts to come back and apologize, and since I'm the kind of cat who always wants to know what is going on, I decided to follow her, and so did Dooley.

We watched her walk off and hit the sidewalk, and saw how Odelia got out of the car and approached the teenager. Aisha broke down, and Odelia wrapped her in her arms.

"She did it!" said Aisha, sniffling.

"Who did what, Aisha?" asked Odelia.

"Layla, of course. I'm sure of it. She killed my brother, and now she's playing the grieving girlfriend."

"But I thought Layla and your brother had broken up?"

"They didn't break up—Todd dumped her. Layla was too needy—he told me so himself. She was crazy. Obsessed. Always sending him messages—up to a hundred a day. And leaving him little notes in his locker, and even writing him letters. She said she couldn't live without him, and finally he'd had enough so he told her he couldn't see her anymore, and that's when she went crazy. Started stalking him everywhere he went."

"So you think she killed him?"

"Of course she did. She once told him: if I can't have you, no one can! Isn't that clear enough? She should be locked up."

"Do you still have those notes and letters?" asked Chase.

"No, Todd threw them all away."

"And what about the messages on his phone?"

"She must have taken his phone and destroyed it. To make sure no one would find out. But I know what she did—and she won't get away with it!" She turned to Chase. "You have to arrest her, Detective Kingsley. She did it—she killed my brother."

"I'm afraid that without any evidence we can't arrest her, Aisha," said Chase.

"What evidence do you need? I'll help you. Ask me anything. I'll help you catch her!"

But when Chase gave her a helpless look, she muttered a loud groan of frustration, then stalked off, angrily swiping at her tears.

"If we could just get our hands on that phone," said Odelia, as she stood looking after Aisha as the girl disappeared around the corner.

"I applied to get access to his phone records," said Chase, "so maybe that will give us something. And I've been working to get access to his phone's backup."

"Is there a backup?"

"Let's hope so, though I'm not holding my breath. His service provider told me to get in touch with Google, but that will take time. Also, since this investigation is now officially closed, I might get some grief from the Chief."

"Even Uncle Alec has to admit that there's more to this case than meets the eye."

"Yeah, after what Aisha just told us, I think I might be able to convince him to reopen the case."

"Though even if Layla wrote him a hundred messages a day, that still doesn't prove she killed him."

"No, but it would give us a reason to question her. I have a feeling she knows more than she's telling us. Scott, too."

They both stood watching the house where now the voice of Scott could be heard, extolling the virtues of his deceased friend.

He sounded sincere enough.

CHAPTER 27

It was time for us to return home. The wake had come to an end, and we hadn't learned much that made us any the wiser as to the circumstances surrounding Todd's death. And as we rode the short distance to Harrington Street, Odelia offered a fresh take on the matter.

"Isn't it possible that Todd killed himself?"

"How do you mean?" asked Chase

"Well, he wasn't doing well in school lately, he'd broken up with Layla, and was being pursued by her, and he missed his real dad, didn't get along with his stepdad. Maybe it all got to be too much, and so he simply jumped into that pool and... didn't come up again."

"It is possible," Chase allowed. "Though not very likely, babe."

"But why not? It happens. People can get into such a funk that they don't know what they're doing. And especially if he'd been drinking and smoking weed. He was in a bad place, and drink and drugs just made it worse."

Honestly, I didn't see it that way. Todd's death raised all kinds of questions, and we all wanted to find the answers.

But suicide? It wasn't impossible, of course, but somehow the idea didn't strike me as the solution to this baffling mystery.

As to what the solution actually was, I have to admit that I was still stumped.

We arrived home to find Gran and Scarlett in conference with Harriet and Brutus. They were all seated around the garden table, with Harriet trying to teach Scarlett the ABC's of felinedom, and judging from the long faces not exactly succeeding!

"Look, if we can't make this work, Baker Street Cats is a lost cause!" said Brutus.

"I know, sweet potato," said Harriet, looking distinctly unhappy, "but what do you want me to do? The woman doesn't even understand the simplest thing!"

"And?" said Odelia. "Have you made progress?"

"It's hopeless," said Gran, throwing up her hands. "I'm ready to give up."

"And me," said Scarlett. "I've been at this all day, and I still don't understand a single syllable!"

"Hel-lo, Scar-lett," said Harriet, drawing the words out.

"Me-ow me-ow," said Scarlett.

"Why is this so hard to understand!"

"Meow meow meow etcetera etcetera etcetera."

"Aaargh!" Harriet cried, and threw up her paws in a fine imitation of Gran's frustration.

"How did it go with you guys?" asked Brutus.

"There was a wake," I said, "and Aisha Bond accused Layla Walcott of killing her brother."

"She did, did she?"

"She says Layla was obsessed with Todd, and couldn't forgive him for breaking up with her. So she killed him."

"You're investigating a murder?" asked Gran.

"What murder?" asked Scarlett.

"According to my uncle it was an accidental drowning,"

Odelia explained as she took a seat at the table. "But we think something more nefarious is going on."

"This is exactly the kind of thing the Baker Street Cats should be investigating," said Brutus. "Only we're not getting anywhere."

"Didn't you mention that Scarlett's cousin could build an app that could translate feline communication?" I asked.

"Yeah, well, he said that's pretty much science fiction at this point. We still need human operators to work as dispatchers and to field the incoming calls from the cats. Which means that Marge, Odelia or Gran have to drop everything and exclusively work for the Baker Street Cats from now on. And none of them are prepared to do that."

"I'm not going to drop my job to work as a cat dispatcher," said Odelia.

"Me neither," said Gran. "So much as it pains me to say, I think your idea is dead in the water, Brutus."

"My idea!" said Brutus. "This was all Harriet's idea!"

"I think you'll find that it was actually Gran's idea," said Harriet frostily.

And while they argued about whose idea it was to start this ill-conceived cat watch, I decided to have a little think, and put my thoughts in order. We were now working on two cases, and both of them were as yet unsolved. How is it possible that two people had died, and we still weren't even close to finding out exactly what had happened?

Of course they were both very different cases, and nowhere near connected or even similar, but still—Hampton Cove isn't a metropolis. It's not a major town where murders happen on every street corner every minute of every day. When a murder does happen, it's so rare and so shocking it still rallies the entire community and puts pressure on law enforcement to come up with answers, and to guarantee that the person or persons responsible are punished to the fullest extent of the law.

"You know," said Scarlett, "you should stop fighting, you guys."

"We're not fighting," said Gran as she gratefully accepted a cup of tea from Chase, who'd put on the kettle and had made everyone a nice cup of the hot beverage.

Marge and Tex had also joined us, and as the sun set, the whole family was seated around the table, enjoying a balmy night.

"I mean, just look at you," said Scarlett.

They looked at each other, a little puzzled by her words.

"Look at who?" asked Marge.

"I think she means you," said Tex.

"Who, me?"

"All of you!" said Scarlett.

"What's your point, Scarlett?" asked Gran.

"You all have each other, a wonderful family, who all love and care for each other. Me? I don't have anyone."

"You have me," Gran pointed out.

"You know what I mean, Vesta."

We all knew what she meant. Scarlett had never married, and as a consequence didn't have kids, or grandkids.

"You have many male... friends," Marge pointed out carefully.

"Oh, please," said Scarlett. "They don't care a hoot about me, those male 'friends' of mine."

"You know we love you, Scarlett," said Odelia, as she gave Gran's friend a smile. "And that you're like family to us."

"And I'm very grateful for that," said Scarlett.

"Yeah, we love you, even though you're lousy at speaking our cats' language," Gran grunted.

They all laughed, and Tex said, "Don't listen to her, Scarlett. I don't speak that language either."

"Or me," said Chase.

"And that's fine," Tex concluded.

"You know that I've always been jealous of you?" said Scarlett, turning to Gran.

"Jealous! Of me!"

"Sure. When I saw what you had, with your husband and your family." She gave a little sigh. "Maybe that's why Jack and I…"

She didn't have to say more. "It's fine," said Gran, placing a hand on her friend's arm. "That's all in the past now."

"I know—and I'm grateful that we put that all behind us."

"You and me both," said Gran.

Dooley was staring at me. "What's wrong, Max?" he asked. "Why are you looking as if you've just seen a ghost?"

"Because I have, Dooley," I said. "I think I've just seen the ghost of Josslyn Aldridge."

"You have?" He glanced around. "Where?"

But it wasn't the literal ghost of Josslyn I had seen, but the proverbial one.

And suddenly, and just like that, the whole puzzle fell into place. And I knew just what needed to be done to catch one very dangerous and extremely ruthless, calculating killer.

CHAPTER 28

We had returned to the Bonds, with Odelia and Chase deciding Todd's parents deserved an update on the investigation. They didn't want to tell the couple that the case had been closed, though, instead assuring them that the investigation was still ongoing, and that new elements had been recently discovered which made it look promising that a break in the case was imminent.

"Right now we're focusing our attention on the tablet computer your son owned, Mrs. Bond," said Chase.

"Tablet? My son didn't have a tablet," said Rosa.

Once again we'd been invited into the Bonds' cozy living room, and even though Rosa looked wan, she was bearing up bravely—especially in light of the big scene her daughter had created at Todd's wake last night.

Aisha wasn't with us—presumably she was upstairs in her room, moping.

"Oh, yes, he most certainly had one," said Chase. "He got it from Scott. It was an old one that belonged to him, and since Scott's parents decided to buy him a new one, he gave his old one to Todd."

"He set it up to sync with his phone and his laptop," Odelia explained, "which will allow us to finally be able to see all the messages he sent and received."

"And the phone calls he made on that fatal night."

"Where is it—this tablet?" asked Tilton, giving us a look of concern. He'd placed a supportive arm around his wife's shoulder.

"We think we might have a line on that," Chase said.

"So you haven't found it yet?" asked Rosa.

"We haven't. But we think we know who might have taken it."

Rosa frowned. "I don't understand…"

"Where is your daughter, Rosa?" asked Odelia abruptly.

"Upstairs in her room," said Rosa. "Why?"

"Could you ask her to come down? We would like to ask her a couple of questions, if that's all right with you."

"Okay," said Rosa, frowning. She got up and bellowed at the foot of the stairs, "Aisha! Come down a minute, will you?"

"I'm busy!" Aisha shouted back.

"It's the police—they want to talk to you!"

There was much stomping of feet again as Aisha came down the stairs, her face a thundercloud.

"What?" she said, crossing her arms across her chest.

"Don't talk to Odelia and Detective Kingsley like that," her mother admonished her. "Now sit down and be polite."

Aisha rolled her eyes in a perfectly practiced gesture, and plunked herself down on the couch. "What do you want?" she asked.

"Please try and take an interest, Aisha," said Tilton. "It's important."

"I know, Tilton," she said. "Todd was my brother, remember?"

"I do remember," said Tilton, cutting a quick glance to Rosa, who shook her head.

"I'll go and check on the baby," she muttered, and hurried up the stairs.

"Aisha, we know about your brother's tablet," said Odelia.

Moments later, Rosa returned, carrying the baby.

"What tablet?" asked Aisha morosely.

"The tablet Todd got from Scott."

"I don't know about any tablet."

"We talked to Scott, and he confirmed that he gave his old iPad to Todd last month. He even helped him set it up so that it synced with his phone and with his laptop."

"So why are you asking me? If it was Scott's tablet, you should ask him."

"Aisha!" said Rosa.

"I'm sorry, Mom, but I don't know anything about a tablet."

"It wasn't amongst his personal effects," said Odelia, "and it wasn't in his room, so do you have any idea where it might be?"

"No idea," said Aisha immediately. "Now can I go? I have tons of homework to finish."

"No, you don't," said Rosa. She turned to Odelia and gave her a look of apology. "We've been keeping her home from school ever since her brother…" She swallowed with difficulty, and her eyes were soon brimming with tears again.

"I still have a ton of homework, Mom," said Aisha. "Even if I don't go to school, I don't want to fall behind."

"It's fine," said Chase, and immediately Aisha shot up from the couch and was stomping up those stairs again. Moments later the door to her room slammed shut, causing both Rosa and Tilton to wince.

"If she keeps this up we'll have to get a new doorframe soon," said Tilton, and I could tell he wasn't kidding.

"Do you think Aisha knows about her brother's tablet?" asked Rosa.

"Yes, I do," said Chase.

"So why is she lying? And where is it?"

"We're not sure. But if maybe you could keep an eye on her for the next couple of days?"

Rosa nodded, and so did Tilton, both looking extremely concerned now.

"Are you saying… that Aisha could be involved with what happened to Todd?" asked Rosa finally, voicing the question that had forced itself to the forefront of her mind.

"It's too soon to tell," said Chase, getting up. "Just keep an eye on her, will you?"

"Yes, of course," said Tilton as he also got up to escort us to the door.

"I can't believe Aisha would do anything to harm her brother," said Rosa. "She and Todd didn't always get along, but she would never do that."

"Unless it was an accident?" Tilton suggested, giving Odelia and Chase a keen look, as if hoping they would confirm or deny the suspicions of him and his wife.

But Chase was as stony-faced as ever, and Odelia's face, too, didn't reveal anything.

And so moments later we were out on the sidewalk again, and I had the impression we'd left behind two very concerned parents, and one very troubled teenager.

CHAPTER 29

It was the morning after the surprise visit of Detective Kingsley and Odelia Kingsley, and the Bond household was in something of a turmoil. Aisha had insisted today was the day she was going back to school, even though her mom insisted she stay home for another couple of days.

"No, Mom, I'll get too much behind if I stay home."

"But, honey, you're not well."

"I'm fine," said Aisha curtly.

"At least wait until after the funeral."

"I want to go now, okay?"

"If she wants to go, maybe we should let her," said Tilton, who was seated at the kitchen counter, reading his paper and sipping from his cup of black coffee.

"Fine," said Rosa with a sigh of resignation.

The baby was in the high chair, being fed by Rosa, while Aisha stuffed her books into her backpack, clearly eager for her life to return to normal as soon as possible.

Amongst the things she stuffed into her backpack was an iPad. She had cleverly tried to conceal that fact, but it's hard to conceal things from two concerned parents, especially parents who have been told by the police detective in charge of the investigation into their son's death to be extra vigilant where their daughter is concerned.

Breakfast over, Tilton got up and grabbed his car keys from the hallway dresser.

"See you, Mom," said Aisha, waving to her mother, who was trying to put more food into the baby's mouth than was smeared all around it.

"Call me if you want me to pick you up, honey," said Rosa.

"I'll be fine," said Aisha, producing one of those eye rolls she'd become so proficient in.

In the car, she placed her backpack in the backseat, then took up position next to her stepdad, and soon they were en route.

"You don't have to act tougher than you are, sweetie," said Tilton. "It's all right if you don't want to go to school."

"It's fine, Tilton," said Aisha as she sagged in her seat and put her feet up on the dash.

Under normal circumstances Tilton would have told her to put her feet down, but these were not normal circumstances, so he didn't say anything, just put the car in gear and then they were off.

"And please call me dad," said Tilton.

"Fine... Dad," said Aisha, sounding even more bratty than usual.

But it was hard on her, of course, losing a brother like that, so Tilton kept his tongue. He and Rosa had agreed to give Aisha all the space she needed, and had even discussed going to a psychologist with the girl. There was a good one they could schedule through the school, and they had the feeling Aisha was probably going to need it.

It was typical, they'd read after consulting Doctor Google, for kids to appear stronger and more brash than they actually were, to suppress their very real feelings of grief. Sooner or later that grief was bound to express itself, when they realized what had happened, and that the brother they loved and cared for was suddenly gone—ripped from their lives through a cruel twist of fate—or the unseen hand of an as yet unknown force of malice that had reached into their lives and turned it upside down and inside out.

They arrived at school and Aisha got out, studiously ignored her stepdad, then disappeared through the school gates.

Tilton glanced back, saw the backpack, and opened the window to yell, "Aisha—your backpack!"

But it was too late—she had already been swallowed up by the swarming mass of kids.

Tilton glanced back at that backpack, shrugged and then drove off.

On his way to work, he passed an abandoned old factory building, and so he steered his car in that direction, underneath the old sign that said that the best wheelbarrows in the world were made there, and swung his car into the old parking lot, which was now rutted and where weeds and tree roots were steadily pushing up the slabs of concrete.

He reached back and took the backpack, frowning when he opened it and saw the iPad. Todd's iPad. The one he hadn't even known existed.

For a moment, he wondered how to proceed, then he made a decision.

He had to think about his family, after all. Todd was gone, but Rosa was there, and Aisha, and the baby.

He simply had to do what needed to be done.

And so he turned the car around and steered it in the direction of the office.

He parked the car in his usual spot, reserved for him. He got out, glanced around for a moment, then took out the hammer he'd taken from the toolshed that morning before ushering Aisha into the car, and quickly smashed the side window of his car. The glass splintered easily, and moments later he was already heading into the building, took another look around, and when he didn't see anything out of the ordinary, proceeded in the direction of the bank of elevators, zooming up to the top floor, a smile of relief on his face.

The smile was quickly wiped from his lips, however, when he walked into his office and found Chase and Odelia Kingsley there waiting for him. Chase was holding up Aisha's backpack, the one Tilton had dumped in a dumpster around the corner just now, and Odelia was holding up the iPad, which he'd destroyed with a rock.

You could see the glass spidering where the rock had hit.

But it was Detective Kingsley's next words that really set the seal on his mood: "Tilton Bond, I'm arresting you for the murders of Josslyn Aldridge, Willie Dornhauser and Todd Bond. I'm also arresting you for the murders of Janice Schiller and Clive Atcheson. You have the right to remain silent, Tilton—or should I say... Ernest?"

EPILOGUE

"Tilton Bond never made his millions in the internet industry. He made it by robbing the bank he worked for and framing his boss, then murdering him in cold blood," I said.

We were in the backyard of the Poole home, where Tex was whipping up some delicious—or not-so-delicious, depending on your culinary taste—treats for us and the rest of the family to gorge on, and where the entire Poole clan had gathered for the feast.

The four of us were seated on the porch swing, resting peacefully after our copious meal, courtesy of Odelia, and the time had finally come to explain all.

I was grateful to find a captive audience in my three friends, and after gathering my thoughts, I was ready to explain my reasoning in this most baffling case, and how I'd finally decided that the three murders that had recently been committed—and the two historical ones—were all linked, and had been committed by the same man.

"So Tilton Bond was a former employee of the bank?" asked Brutus, trying to wrap his head around this surprising fact.

"Indeed he was," I said. "His real name is Ernest Sarisky, and he was one of those invisible people you find in every company. It was actually Chase who put me on the right track, when he admitted he didn't recognize a colleague of his when we were doing those house-to-house interviews the other day. But even invisible people have their hopes and dreams, even if nobody notices them or pays them any attention, and Ernest's hopes and dreams were one day to be like his boss, Clive Atcheson. He'd long harbored a powerful resentment toward Clive. Or perhaps pathological jealousy would be a better term to describe his feelings toward the bank's popular branch manager. And it's not difficult to see why: Clive Atcheson was everything that Ernest was not: he was wealthy, handsome, had a wonderful family, and was well-liked by all. Ernest, on the other hand, was eking out a meager existence on a modest salary, had never been able to attract the attention of a woman, and was a miserable, lonely and bitter man."

"Not really a fun guy, was he?" said Dooley.

"No, Dooley, he certainly was not," I agreed.

"He must have felt really bad," said Harriet, "with nobody noticing him and all. I can imagine how he must have suffered."

It was clear she felt for Ernest. Then of course Harriet would also suffer tremendously if no one noticed her, so she could relate to the man's torment.

"But that all changed the day he woke up with an exciting idea. He was going to steal Clive's perfect life: his money, his family—everything. It was a crazy idea, but he was fed up with being a nobody, and put a plan in motion to become a somebody, whatever it took."

"And it took a lot of bloodshed," said Dooley quietly.

"So Clive Atcheson never escaped to Mexico?" asked Brutus. "With five million?"

"No, he didn't," I said. "We now know that Clive Atcheson, and his secretary Janice Schiller, were killed on the same day the bank was robbed." Ernest was fully cooperating with the police, and they now had a pretty good idea about what happened. After taking the money from the vault, he forced Clive and Janice Schiller at gunpoint into a boat he'd rented under an alias, and once they were out on the open ocean, he killed them both and dumped their bodies overboard.

"But what happened to Ernest?" asked Harriet. "How did he explain his sudden disappearance?"

"After the robbery, justifiably there was a lot of confusion. Ernest simply quit his job, announced that he was moving out of state to be closer to his aging parents, and that was it. Nobody cared and nobody asked any questions. He was the invisible man, remember?"

"But in actual fact he changed his name and moved to Hampton Cove?"

"Not immediately. First he needed to wait and see what Rosa would do. He assumed she wouldn't want to stay in Wilmington, to avoid the scandal and the gossip, and he was right. He'd planted certain evidence to make it look as if Clive and Janice were having an affair—love letters, doctored photos and hotel room bookings—and that they planned to head across the border after the heist. So Rosa changed her identity, moved to Hampton Cove and started a new life."

"And then suddenly Tilton Bond entered the scene," said Harriet.

"Indeed. Ernest, having assumed a new identity, 'accidentally' ran into Rosa in town, and started pursuing her with a vigor that must have left her breathless. And for a woman whose husband had betrayed her as she thought Clive had done, being courted like that must have felt very comforting. She quickly confided in Tilton, and soon he became her confidant. Her rock. Let's not forget that she was vulnerable after Clive's alleged betrayal."

"A position Tilton had put her in."

"But didn't she recognize him from the bank?" asked Brutus. "They must have met at office parties, right?"

"Oh, no doubt they had, but like I said, Tilton had been one of those people nobody pays any attention to. He could just as well not have been there. And also, he'd changed his appearance. He used to be a man with a receding hairline and a weak chin, but now he had a full crop of hair and a fashionable beard. He'd been overweight, but now he was athletic, taking full benefit of his gym membership. In other words: a changed man."

"A millionaire!" said Dooley.

"Wealth lends a person a certain aura. And it was this aura that surrounded Tilton."

"Okay, so why did he kill that poor woman on the beach?" asked Harriet.

"Josslyn Aldridge wasn't just any woman. She was an ex-colleague of his. It hadn't hit me when I studied the pictures of Rosa and her husband, but when I looked at them again, there he was, Tilton Bond. In the background, hardly noticeable. I thought he was looking at Janice in that picture, but in actual fact he was looking at Rosa. But then I also noticed Josslyn. And when you look closely, you can see that Josslyn has the same look in her eyes that Tilton had. But where Tilton is looking at Rosa, she is actually looking at Tilton."

"She was in love with him?" asked Harriet.

"She was. Even invisible people have people who are in love with them, only they're too obsessed with the ones they can't have to notice. But Josslyn wanted him just as much as he wanted Rosa. And so all these many years later, when she bumped into him, she immediately recognized him as her old colleague Ernest. And of course he couldn't have that.

She would have jeopardized everything he'd worked so hard to achieve."

"Everything he'd killed to achieve, you mean," Brutus grunted.

"So he killed Josslyn? Just like that?" asked Dooley.

"Yes, he did. He arranged to meet her that evening on the beach, and killed her. Josslyn must have been so happy—so thrilled to finally meet him again—the colleague she'd loved from afar all those years. She didn't have a clue her fate was sealed the moment he laid eyes on her and saw that she recognized him. He then made it look like a mugging by grabbing her purse, removing her wallet and dumping her purse in the sand."

"So what about the blackmailer?" asked Harriet. "Why did he kill him?"

"Willie Dornhauser had seen Chase's appeal for witnesses in Josslyn's mugging, and had googled Josslyn. I think he must have hit on the same picture I saw, and immediately recognized Rosa. He then did some digging, and discovered that Rosa's husband was actually the infamous Clive Atcheson, who'd absconded with five million dollars, and figured here was an opportunity to make some money."

"So he put the squeeze on Rosa," said Brutus, nodding.

"Only Tilton realized that if this guy had discovered his wife's true identity, it was only a matter of time before he put two and two together, and discovered his identity as well. So the night the money was to change hands, Tilton was also in the park, watching and waiting. And when Willie showed up, he followed him home and killed him on the spot."

"But why didn't he take the money?" asked Harriet.

"I think Edwardo showed up and Tilton had to flee the scene before he could search the house. And in a way, that actually worked out even better for him, since Edwardo took the money, and in the process set himself up as the perfect suspect."

"He was very lucky," said Dooley.

"He was, until Todd started digging into his past life, and discovering certain things."

"Todd found out who he really was?" asked Harriet.

I nodded. "Todd had also seen Chase's appeal."

"Looks like that appeal made a big difference!" said Dooley.

"It did. What actually happened was that the Bonds had watched that appeal together, as a family."

"Just like we did!"

"And Rosa recognized Josslyn, and mentioned something about her being an ex-colleague of her husband's. And Todd being Todd, and always eager to find out anything he could about his real dad, started surfing the web, looking up Josslyn. And that's when he recognized his stepdad as also being one of his real dad's colleagues."

"That must have been a great shock to him," said Harriet.

"Yes, it was. He confronted his stepdad, and accused him of knowing what had happened to his dad, and maybe even lying to protect him. He might have even believed that Tilton and Clive had set up that bank heist together, and split the money."

"So he didn't realize the ugly truth, that his stepdad had killed his real dad."

"No, he didn't. But he was getting close. Too close. He had a big fight with his stepdad, with Todd demanding to know where his dad was, and how he could get in touch with him, and that's when Todd walked out and went to stay with his best friend Scott."

"But he didn't tell Scott," said Brutus.

"Or Layla," said Harriet.

"No, I think he was ashamed of what his dad had done,

and didn't want them to know. Also, he wanted to protect the family's new identity. If it became known that he was the son of an infamous bank robber, their life in Hampton Cove was over. So he kept quiet, but he also kept digging."

"So that's why he was so withdrawn and irritable," said Harriet.

"I think he must have reconstructed some sort of theory in his head, and that's when he set up a meeting with his stepdad, to pressure him into telling him the truth. Though I'm pretty sure that all he wanted was to get in touch with his dad in Mexico."

"So he met Tilton that night by the pool? At the Walcotts?"

"Yes. Todd waited until Scott and Layla had gone to bed, then called Tilton and arranged to meet. And that's when Tilton killed his stepson, and took his phone and laptop."

"But the man is a cold-blooded murderer, Max!" said Dooley.

"Oh, yes, he is. To protect his secret, he was prepared to do whatever it took, even murdering his stepson."

"So that's the screaming and the splashing Mr. Durain heard?"

"Yes. And if Lionel Durain would have taken a look through his window, he would have caught Todd's killer."

"Tilton was taking an awfully big risk," said Harriet.

"He was. He was getting more and more desperate at this point. And a desperate man is a dangerous man, especially a calculating killer like him."

"But how did you get onto him, Max?" asked Dooley. "How did you catch him?"

"Well, it was actually Scarlett who put me on the right track."

"Scarlett? Did she finally manage to talk to you?" asked Brutus with a frown.

"No, she didn't. But you'll remember that she sat down with Gran, and said that Gran didn't know how lucky she was to have such a great family. And how she wished her own life could have been different. And I don't know why, but I suddenly flashed back to that picture of Rosa and Clive at that Christmas party, and the wistful glances Tilton kept darting at her. Here was a man who clearly wished he had the life she and Clive were leading. I also remembered Chase's invisible colleague, and so when I went back to that picture, I suddenly recognized Tilton, and when I looked a little closer, I also saw Josslyn."

"Odd that no one had ever bothered to examine that picture," said Harriet.

"I hadn't noticed it either," I said. "Unless you know what to look for, it's hard to see. Even Willie Dornhauser hadn't recognized Tilton."

"Todd recognized him."

"Yes, but that's because Todd had been living with Tilton, seeing him every day. And even he didn't see the truth, even when it was staring him in the face."

"Rosa would have known," said Harriet. "She would have seen through Tilton's deception."

"That's what Tilton was afraid of," I said, nodding, "and why Todd had to die. But I'm not so sure. Tilton is a skilled liar. I'm sure he would have come up with a convincing story, and maybe Rosa would have fallen for it. Then again, maybe she wouldn't have."

"So what was this business with the iPad all about?" asked Brutus.

I smiled. "That's just something I came up with. Todd never had an iPad. But it was important to make Tilton believe that he had, and that it contained incriminating evidence—like the messages he and his stepson exchanged. So that iPad had to disappear."

"And Aisha was in on the plan?"

"She was—though we never told her what it was all about. Just that she needed to put the iPad we gave her in her backpack and make sure that Tilton saw her do it, then leave her backpack in the car. And then once the bait was placed, all we had to do was see if Tilton took it. And he did. He tried to destroy the iPad and make it look as if thieves had broken into his car and snatched it."

"Just like with Josslyn's purse."

I nodded. "He put up a fight when they grabbed him, but it was just a token fight. I think at that point he knew the game was over. Chase said he even looked relieved when he finally confessed. Nine years he'd been living with that secret, and all this time he must have lived in fear that someone would recognize him and the whole house of cards would come crashing down."

"And then suddenly it did," said Brutus.

"He must have been very upset when Josslyn recognized him," said Dooley.

"It gave him the shock of a lifetime," I said. "The one thing he'd been afraid of all this time, looking over his shoulder to avoid, suddenly happened. And it was the beginning of the end for him."

"So what's going to happen now?" asked Harriet. "Will Rosa have to change her name again and move to another town?"

"I don't think so," I said. "Now that the whole truth is known, and it has become obvious that her first husband was framed, she doesn't have to hide anymore."

"She will be poor again, though," said Harriet. "All that money Tilton stole will have to be returned to the bank."

"So she'll get a job. It's better than believing that your husband is a bank robber and left you for his secretary."

"I think they'll be just fine," said Dooley, the eternal optimist. "And she can always write a book about what happened. People love those true crime stories. Or start a podcast!"

"A podcast?" asked Harriet.

"Oh, yes," I said. "True crime podcasts are all the rage right now."

"They are, huh?" She cut a quick glance to her boyfriend, who was tackling a particularly chewy piece of meat. "Did you hear that, angel face? True crime podcasts are all the rage right now. Lots of money to be made."

Brutus abruptly stopped chewing the meat—it was to no avail anyway, as it was charred to a crisp. "Money?" he said, perking up at the delicious sound of the word.

"So maybe we should do a podcast," said Harriet. "We have plenty of true crime experience, being part of this town's leading team of detectives."

"You'd still need a human to host it," I pointed out. "Same as with your, um, Baker Street Cats project."

"How is that going, Harriet?" asked Dooley innocently.

"It's not," Harriet snapped. She then gave me a sweet look. "Max? Why don't you give us the skinny on all the cases you've worked, and we'll ask Scarlett to read them out in our new podcast?"

"Scarlett again?" I said. "So she's able to speak our language now, is she?"

"No, she's not."

"Hopeless case, that one," Brutus grumbled, making a throwaway gesture with his paw.

"But she does have a great voice," said Harriet. "And so I was thinking—"

"We were thinking," Brutus corrected her.

"That maybe you could tell your stories to Odelia, and then Odelia could type them up and Scarlett could read them on this podcast thingy."

"Why are you asking me?" I said. "You know the stories just as well as I do."

"Well, there is the small matter of royalties," Harriet said.

"We'll share them," said Brutus. "Equal shares for all of us."

"Oh, goodie," said Dooley.

"Not you, Dooley," Brutus grunted. "You're not a part of this."

"You're the invisible cat, Dooley," I quipped.

"Just so," said Brutus. "So that's fifty percent for me, and fifty percent for Harriet, and…" He frowned. "Mh. There seems to be something wrong with my math."

"Oh, Brutus, baby doodle, it's simple. Max gets ten percent as the original author, and the rest is to be divided between us as the podcast creators."

"And Scarlett?" I asked. "Doesn't she get anything?"

"Oh, she'll do it for the exposure," said Harriet. "And so will Odelia. This will be great for that little paper of hers."

And so Brutus and Harriet took off, to discuss the terms of their new podcast deal, and Dooley and I laid down our heads and decided to have a little postprandial nap.

"What are the chances that this new podcast will take off, Max?" asked Dooley.

"About as much as they're willing to offer Scarlett and Odelia," I said, yawning. "In other words: zero."

"It doesn't seem fair, Max."

"What doesn't, Dooley?"

"Well, you're the one who solves all these murders, and the only ones who get credit for it are Odelia, Chase and Uncle Alec."

"That's life, Dooley," I said. "Besides, I don't need credit. As long as I get plenty of kibble and cuddles, I'm a happy cat."

"Still, it doesn't seem right."

I just shrugged. Dooley might have a point, but frankly I

didn't really care about fair. As long as the people who had committed these terrible crimes got their just reward, it was fine by me. But then someone shouted my name, and when I opened my eyes, I saw that all the humans around the table had raised their glasses, and were toasting… me!

"To Max!" said Odelia. "The greatest cat detective ever!"

"To Max!" the others all chimed in.

"Oh, you guys," I muttered, and I may or may not have teared up at this point.

Okay, so I do like to get the credit.

What do you expect?

I'm only feline, after all.

THE END

Thanks for reading! If you want to know when a new Nic Saint book comes out, sign up for Nic's mailing list: nicsaint.com/news

EXCERPT FROM PURRFECT THIEF (MAX 43)

Prologue

Rudyard van de Graaf, patriarch of the well-known van de Graaf family, had a habit, developed over the years, where he liked to savor all the things in life he enjoyed the most. In no particular order these were: a good cigar, an excellent malt whiskey, and of course his rare collection of exquisite art, acquired over a lifetime of diligent collecting. And since he was about to celebrate his eighty-sixth birthday next week, he'd managed to cram a whole lot of collecting into such a long life. He would have included women in the list of things he enjoyed, but ever since his wife Mimi had passed away, he'd decided to forego this particular pleasure, and do without female company.

And so he sat, smoking a fine cigar, sampling a vintage whiskey, and admiring the pride of his collection: the rare and invaluable Drossart Dagger. A gift from a good friend—long since deceased—it held pride of place in what he called his treasure chest, a small room adjacent to his study, where

EXCERPT FROM PURRFECT THIEF (MAX 43)

he kept the crème de la crème of his collection. An art historian, were he allowed access to Rudyard's inner sanctum, would probably be stunned when he saw the things that were gathered there in this one room. From valuable paintings, to rare pieces of China, to an entire glass cabinet filled with jewelry that had been worn by kings and queens—in fact very few mortals had ever enjoyed the pleasure of laying eyes on the rare pieces on display—all reserved for the eyes of one man only.

Rudyard hummed a contented tune as he rose from his armchair with a groan and admired his Drossart Dagger up close. The hilt of the dagger had been inset with rubies and diamonds and other precious stones, and the blade itself was as sharp now as it had been when first forged in the fires of ancient Babylon, or at least that's what the legend held. Whether it was true or not, Rudyard didn't give a damn. All he cared about was that it was as mythical as the dodo egg, and most importantly, that it was his and his alone.

Mashing out his cigar in the ashtray, and taking his tumbler into the living area of his apartment and placing it on the tray, to be carried away in the morning by a member of his household staff, he carefully closed and locked the door to his treasure room, placed the key in the top drawer of a nearby cabinet, then started preparations to turn in for the night. Half an hour later, all was quiet in the apartment, and only the regular breathing of Rudyard could be heard, interspersed with an occasional whistling sound escaping his old lungs, coated in the tar of a thousand cigars.

And Rudyard had just been dreaming about participating in a game of golf and coming out on top, as usual, when suddenly he was stirred from his dream by the sound of a click.

Instantly wide awake, he glanced around, for he'd recognized that click. It was the sound a particular wall panel made when returning to its usual position.

Odd, he thought. Almost as if… And as a sudden premonition took hold of him, he was out of his bed with an anxious snarl, shoving his feet into his velvet slippers and hurrying into his study. Glancing over to the door of his treasure room, his heart leaped into his throat and promptly collided with his uvula when he saw that the door… was ajar!

"No!" he gurgled as emotions too powerful for speech fought for prevalence in his bosom. And as he thrust open the door, the first place his eyes landed on was the glass display cabinet where his Drossart Dagger usually resided. But the dagger… was gone!

Chapter One

Humans have many ways to pass the time: playing tennis, working out at the gym, dancing at a club, watching television, going to the cinema, or simply putting in their eight hours at the job and coming home to do the busywork associated with running a household. Cats, on the other hand, have only one pastime, and that is napping. It's cheap, it's easy, and anyone can do it. And, best of all, it provides you with free entertainment in the form of dreams. Yes, cats do dream. Mostly of our next meal, or, as the case may be, our next nap. So as you see, the life of your feline companion is fairly straightforward.

Except of course for this particular feline, since my human's job consists of writing stories for a living for our local newspaper, and investigating those stories and even digging deep into the kinds of mysteries that seem to plague her fellow man or woman.

And it was exactly such a case that presented itself to her when her boss Dan Goory ushered a young man and a young

EXCERPT FROM PURRFECT THIEF (MAX 43)

woman into her office—and immediately I knew that nap time was over, and that an interesting new situation was about to unfold.

For the young woman was none other than Casey van de Graaf, and the young man Zalman Mulhearn. If these names mean nothing to you, then you probably haven't read the society section of the newspaper lately, for they both hail from families as prominent as it gets. Both the van de Graaf and Mulhearn family tree go back a couple of hundred years, which is also the point in time their forebears made their fortune, and have passed said fortune onto future generations who, contrary to some, have managed not only to maintain but to increase that fortune manyfold. In other words: they're outrageously rich.

Harriet, for one, pricked up her ears immediately when the young people arrived. Harriet is my white Persian friend, and had been dozing peacefully in a corner of the office. Money means everything to Harriet, and so does social standing, and here were the scions of two families who possessed both of those much-coveted traits.

Brutus, Harriet's mate, didn't stir. The butch black cat much prefers napping to having to listen to people gab about their problems, as most people who enter Odelia's office are wont to do. And then of course there was Dooley, my best friend and comrade. He, too, had noticed the sudden intrusion upon the peace and quiet by these newcomers.

He yawned and stretched and said, "Who are these two, Max?"

"If I'm not mistaken, Dooley," I said, "and I don't think I am, these are the harbingers of something new and exciting."

"Representatives of a kibble company, are they?"

"Not exactly," I said, and glanced over to Odelia, wondering if she, too, had recognized the pair.

"Hi," said the girl, holding out a polite hand and shaking

Odelia's. "My name is Casey van de Graaf, and this is Zalman Mulhearn." She glanced over to the young man, who nodded encouragingly, as if to say: you do the talking, and I'll fill in the gaps if need be.

"Yes, of course," said Odelia. "You're the daughter of Royden van de Graaf, aren't you?"

"You know my dad?" asked the girl, much surprised.

"I interviewed him once," said Odelia, gesturing for the duo to take a seat, which they promptly did. "For our series on the great families of Hampton Cove."

"Then you probably know my parents, too," said Zalman.

"Yes, as a matter of fact I do," said Odelia with a smile. "Now how can I help you?"

"Well, the thing is, Mrs. Kingsley," said Casey, glancing to Zalman, "that we find ourselves in something of a pickle."

"So they're not kibble salespeople?" asked Dooley.

"No, Dooley, they're not," I said. "In fact I don't think they're here to sell something, but to ask for something." And Casey's next words bore this out.

"You see, Zalman and I are supposed to get married,'" said Casey.

"Oh, congratulations," said Odelia.

"No, the thing is that we don't want to get married."

"You don't?"

"Well, at least not to each other." She gave a nervous laugh. "It's a little complicated, I'm afraid."

She was very beautiful, this Casey van de Graaf, with long blond hair and refined features. Zalman, too, was no slouch in the looks department. He, too, was blond, and his face looked as if hewn from the living rock. Adonis would have been jealous had he made Zalman's acquaintance. In fact they looked as if they could have been brother and sister. And for a moment I couldn't help but wonder what kind of kids these

EXCERPT FROM PURRFECT THIEF (MAX 43)

two would put on the planet if they did get married. Perfect kids, most probably.

"So you want to get married, but not to each other?" asked Odelia, who looked intrigued at this point, as was I.

"Yes, you see, our families want us to get married, but we don't."

"There's an arrangement," said Zalman, speaking up for the first time. "An arrangement between our families for us to get married."

"The arrangement was made a long time ago," Casey picked up the tale. "Before we were born, in fact. You see, we're almost the same age, Zalman and I."

"You're a week older than me," said Zalman with a smile.

"Barely a week," said Casey, returning the smile and placing a hand on Zalman's arm. If these two weren't a couple, they definitely were close friends, that much was obvious.

"So an arrangement was made?" asked Odelia. "What kind of arrangement?"

Casey took a deep breath. "The thing is that our families are amongst the most prominent… in the state, probably. Maybe even the country."

"Not probably—definitely," Zalman corrected her.

"Well, yes, and so when our respective moms were pregnant with us, our grandads, who have always been friends, decided that the two families should be united by a wedding. And so they arranged for the two newborn babies one day to get married and in this way join the families together into one family."

"And you are those babies?" asked Odelia.

"Yes. This was twenty-five years ago now, and our grandfathers have decided that the time has come for us to honor the arrangement."

"But that's crazy," said Odelia.

EXCERPT FROM PURRFECT THIEF (MAX 43)

"I know, right?" said Casey. "But there it is."

"It's not that I don't like Casey, Mrs. Kingsley," said Zalman, "because I do. In fact she's one of my closest friends."

"But we don't love each other," said Casey. "Not in that way at least. In fact I've been seeing someone for some time now, and we very much would like to get married."

"Same here," said Zalman. "I've been dating a girl for the past five years."

"Only we can't, you see?" said Casey.

"Because of this arrangement," said Odelia, nodding. "But what's stopping you from simply going to your grandfathers and telling them that you don't intend to honor an arrangement that has nothing to do with you? I mean, this isn't the Middle Ages. People should be free to marry whoever they want."

"Oh, I know, and I agree with you completely," said Casey. "But the problem is that my grandfather has made certain stipulations to ensure that this wedding will go through."

"What stipulations?"

Casey shuffled in her chair. "You will treat this discreetly, won't you, Mrs. Kingsley?"

"Of course."

"Well, my grandfather has made a will," said Casey, "that stipulates that when the wedding takes place, his son—my dad—inherits. But if there is no wedding, everything will go to a charity of my grandfather's choosing. And I do mean everything."

"What charity?" asked Odelia with a frown.

"Oh, I'm sure there are several."

"So… that means that if you don't get married, your family…"

"Will be poor as church mice," said Casey, nodding. She took a deep breath. "Also, my grandfather is turning eighty-six next week, and he has said that if he dies before the wedding vows have been exchanged, the same principle applies: the family holding and all the family assets will be liquidated and everything donated to charity."

Odelia sat back. "Now that's something I've never heard before."

"No, my grandfather is what you might call an eccentric," said Casey with a nervous little laugh.

"And what about your grandfather, Zalman?" asked Odelia. "Has he made the same kind of will?"

"No, as far as I know he hasn't. He would very much like for us to get married, sure, but he hasn't made it a condition of his will as far as I know."

"In other words, he's not as crazy as my grandad," said Casey.

"Do you think he's for real?" asked Odelia.

"Oh, yes," said Casey, nodding with a grim look on her face. "Believe me, Mrs. Kingsley, my grandfather is very much for real. And if you knew him, you would understand."

"He's a serious-minded person," said Zalman. "And if I'm honest, a little scary, too."

"Or a lot scary," said Casey. "I know that when I was little, I was always scared of my grandad."

"Wow," said Odelia, and that was probably the most appropriate response.

"I know, right? So..." She glanced to her friend, who had just discovered that the office also seemed to be the home of no less than four cats. "Zalman?" asked Casey.

"Yes," said the young man, dragging his eyes away from four pairs of cat eyes regarding him very closely. He cleared his throat. "So we were wondering, Mrs. Kingsley..."

"If maybe you could have a chat with my grandfather?"

"And make him see the error of his ways."

EXCERPT FROM PURRFECT THIEF (MAX 43)

"He won't listen to me," said Casey. "And he won't listen to my mom and dad."

"So we thought that maybe he might listen to an outsider. Someone not connected to either family."

"You mean try and shame him into changing his viewpoint?" asked Odelia.

Casey grimaced. "Something like that. You see, my grandad is very sensitive to the opinion of others. So we thought that if you were to approach him, he might see reason."

"Because if that doesn't work," said Zalman, "we just might have to get married after all."

"We could get married," said Casey, "and then wait for my grandfather to pass away, and get divorced."

"That sounds a little harsh," said Odelia with a surprised laugh.

"I know, but at this point we're both desperate."

"It was actually my grandfather's suggestion," said Zalman.

"Oh, so your grandfather…"

Zalman nodded. "He's on our side. He realizes that this is just crazy."

"Has he talked to your grandfather, Casey?"

"He has, but my grandad isn't budging. In fact since Zalman's grandfather had a talk with him, he refuses to have anything more to do with him. Says the old man has lost his marbles and must have gone mad, to change his view like that."

"He called him a traitor," said Zalman dryly.

"The problem is—and I know this sounds bad—that my grandad is in great health."

"So he might live another ten or twenty years," said Odelia, nodding.

"Maybe not twenty, but ten or fifteen? Absolutely. His

doctor says he's got the heart of a man half his age." She glanced to Zalman. "And even though Zalman is a great friend, I don't want to stay married to him for ten or fifteen years, and ask my boyfriend to wait that long."

"Same here," said Zalman.

"You could of course get married, and in the meantime…" Odelia began

But both young people shook their heads decidedly. "I know what you're saying," said Casey, "and that's out of the question. My boyfriend wouldn't go for it. In fact I'd probably lose him. And also, what would people think? And what if we want to have kids?"

"Yeah, that plan pretty much went out the window the moment we thought of it," Zalman concurred.

"So you see?" said Casey. "We're at the end of our rope here."

"We don't know what else to do," Zalman said.

"There's no guarantee that your grandad will listen to me," said Odelia. "In fact the more you tell me about him the more I'm inclined to think he'll simply kick me out."

"He won't do that," said Casey decidedly. She turned to Zalman. "Will he?"

Zalman shrugged. "Anything is possible with your grandad, Case."

"Look, I'm willing to give it a try," said Odelia.

"Oh, please do, Mrs. Kingsley," said Casey, intertwining her fingers into a pleading gesture.

"And if that doesn't work?" said Zalman. "We can always threaten to jump off a roof together."

Chapter Two

The drive over to the large mansion that housed the van de Graaf clan was a short one—the advantage of living in a

EXCERPT FROM PURRFECT THIEF (MAX 43)

small town like Hampton Cove. Much to our surprise, though, the drive of the house was filled with police cars, and cops were swarming around as if a police convention was being hosted inside.

"What's going on here?" asked Odelia, visibly surprised that something was happening that she didn't know about.

We approached the house, and as we walked in, Odelia's husband came walking out!

"Fancy meeting you here," said Chase with a big grin.

"What's going on?" asked Odelia.

"I assumed you knew. Why else are you here?"

"I'm here to talk to Rudyard van de Graaf."

"Yeah, well, take a number," said Chase, gesturing to the cops milling about.

"He's not…"

"Dead? Oh, no. John Robie might be a nuisance, but he's definitely not a killer."

"John Robie?"

"Yeah, that's what we've decided to call him." When she continued to stare at him, he added, "The cat burglar? This is his fourth burglary in two weeks, and frankly your uncle is getting fed up with his antics."

"Oh, the cat burglar!" said Odelia, understanding finally dawning.

"Yeah, the cat burglar," said Chase. "I thought you were here for the break-in?"

"No, there's something else I need to speak to him about."

Chase waited for her to clarify, but when no explanations followed, he asked, "What?"

"I'll tell you later if that's all right with you," she said, giving him a kiss on the cheek. "Where can I find him?"

"Take the main staircase and keep going until you reach the top. That's where you'll find the old guy. Or you could take the elevator, but we've been told that's for private use

EXCERPT FROM PURRFECT THIEF (MAX 43)

only, and the housekeeper said that the old man is fussy about who uses his elevator."

"The staircase it is," said Odelia, then turned to us. "Follow me, you guys. Looks like we're moving up in the world."

"Oh, no," I muttered. I don't know about you, but I just hate staircases. It's easy for humans, because they're big, and staircases are made for them, but for us cats it's hard work to navigate all those stairs.

"What's the matter, Maxie, baby?" asked Brutus with a sneer in his voice. "Too lazy to take the stairs?"

"Not too lazy," I said. "But you have to admit it is hard work."

"I'm not admitting any such thing," said Brutus, who's something of an athlete. "Here, I'll show you how it's done," he said, and started running up those stairs as if it was an Olympic discipline and he just had to win the gold. He's like that, you see. Competitive.

Harriet, too, moved up those stairs with swift movements —even a certain grace. And then it was just me and Dooley. The stragglers, as usual.

"Let's go, Dooley," I said with a weary sigh. "I just wish they'd install elevators for cats."

"Is that a thing?" asked Dooley, much interested. He's a smallish cat, and with his short legs it's even harder for him to move up a staircase.

"I'm not sure," I said, "but if it's not, someone should invent one. I'm sure there's a big market for it."

"Or we could ask one of these nice cops to pick us up and carry us up the stairs," he suggested.

He was probably right. Cops were going up and down the stairs all the time. One of them could easily have picked us up. But unfortunately none of them spoke our language, and

EXCERPT FROM PURRFECT THIEF (MAX 43)

no matter how piteously I regarded them, even producing a sad meow, they all chose to ignore me.

So finally I decided that the best way to deal with the obstacle was simply to tackle it. Also, there was no alternative.

Sixty steps. That's how many steps we needed to climb before we reached the top of the house. Sixty! The people who design these places are definitely cat haters. There can be no doubt. Only a cat hater would put us through so much misery to go anywhere.

Finally we made it, and even though I was hot and out of breath, I couldn't help but notice that the target of Odelia's negotiations was in no mood to listen to her right now.

The old man sat in a nice comfy armchair, watching the goings-on with an incandescent eye, and when Odelia approached him and introduced herself, he waved an irritable hand and said, "I've got no time for that nonsense."

"But Casey specifically asked me to—"

"I don't care!" he bellowed. "Have you found my collection yet? No? Well, as long as you don't get me my stuff back I don't care what Casey wants or doesn't want."

"What's missing?" asked Odelia, changing tack.

"None of your business," growled the old man.

"Excuse me?"

"Fine, consider yourself excused. Now please go. And leave me to mourn in peace."

"But sir—"

"Go! Isn't it bad enough that I was robbed last night? Do you want me to die from high blood pressure by having to shout at you? No? Well, then leave. Now!"

And so Odelia walked out, her mission a big bust.

"I think we better come back later," she announced.

"Sometimes a strategic retreat is the best option," I

EXCERPT FROM PURRFECT THIEF (MAX 43)

concurred, but then I remembered those stairs. "Oh, God, no," I muttered as I stared into the abyss. If you think going up is hard for a cat, imagine how much harder it is to go down!

"Here, I'll carry you," said Odelia, and picked me up. "You, too, Dooley."

I don't think I've ever loved any human more than I did Odelia right then.

ABOUT NIC

Nic has a background in political science and before being struck by the writing bug worked odd jobs around the world (including but not limited to massage therapist in Mexico, gardener in Italy, restaurant manager in India, and Berlitz teacher in Belgium).

When he's not writing he enjoys curling up with a good (comic) book, watching British crime dramas, French comedies or Nancy Meyers movies, sampling pastry (apple cake!), pasta and chocolate (preferably the dark variety), twisting himself into a pretzel doing morning yoga, going for a brisk walk, and spoiling his feline assistants Lily and Ricky.

He lives with his wife (and aforementioned cats) in a small village smack dab in the middle of absolutely nowhere and is probably writing his next 'Mysteries of Max' book right now.

www.nicsaint.com

Made in the USA
Monee, IL
04 March 2025